Gérard de Villiers

SURFACE TO AIR

Gérard de Villiers (1929–2013) is the most popular writer of spy thrillers in French history. His two-hundred-odd books about the adventures of Austrian nobleman and freelance CIA operative Malko Linge have sold millions of copies.

Linge, who first appeared in 1965, has often been compared to Ian Fleming's hero James Bond. The two secret agents share a taste for gunplay and kinky sex, but de Villiers was a journalist at heart, and his books are based on constant travel and reporting in dozens of countries.

On several occasions de Villiers was even ahead of the news. His 1980 novel had Islamists killing President Anwar el-Sādāt of Egypt a year before the event took place. *The Madmen of Benghazi* described CIA involvement in Libya long before the 2012 attack on the Benghazi compound. In *Surface to Air*, an interagency rivalry draws the FBI and the CIA into the world of black-market arms sales, corruption, and death in Russia and the Caucasus.

SURFACE TO AIR

SURFACE TO AIR

A MALKO LINGE NOVEL

Gérard de Villiers

Translated from the French by William Rodarmor

Vintage Crime/Black Lizard

Vintage Books

A Division of Penguin Random House LLC | New York

FIRST VINTAGE CRIME/BLACK LIZARD OPEN-MARKET EDITION, SEPTEMBER 2016

Translation copyright © 2016 by William Rodarmor

All rights reserved. Published in the United States by Vintage Books, a division of Penguin Random House LLC, New York. Originally published in France as *Igla S* by Éditions Gérard de Villiers, Paris, in 2012. Copyright © 2012 by Éditions Gérard de Villiers.

Vintage is a registered trademark and Vintage Crime/Black Lizard and colophon are trademarks of Penguin Random House LLC.

This is a work of fiction. Names, characters, places, and incidents either are the product of the author's imagination or are used fictitiously. Any resemblance to actual persons, living or dead, events, or locales is entirely coincidental.

The Cataloging-in-Publication data is on file at the Library of Congress.

Vintage Books Open-Market ISBN: 978-0-804-16939-4
eBook ISBN: 978-0-804-16940-0

Book design by Joy O'Meara

www.weeklylizard.com

Printed in the United States of America

10 9 8 7 6 5 4 3 2 1

SURFACE TO AIR

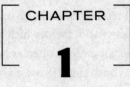

New Jersey

Parviz Amritzar was looking at Benazir but with-out seeing her. His eyes were locked on the telephone on the night table next to the bed.

"What's the matter with you?" she asked in Urdu.

This wasn't the first time he had taken his young wife to a hotel, but they usually started making love as soon as they got to their room. This time was different. For one thing, the Newark Liberty hotel was unusually charmless. It stood less than a mile from the airport runways and featured white walls decorated with banal prints and windows double-glazed against the aircraft noise. For another, Amritzar seemed distracted.

A good wife who never questioned her husband, Benazir didn't ask why Amritzar had taken her to this cheesy place. They usually crossed the Hudson to spend

3

weekends at one of the boutique hotels on the West Side of Manhattan.

Amritzar had recently brought his aged mother from Pakistan to come live with them, which tended to inhibit his sex life. So he got away as often as he could to enjoy his wife without constraint. He was a wholesale oriental carpet dealer, earned a good living, and, aside from making a good Muslim's *zakat* alms, had few expenses.

"I'm expecting a phone call here," he told Benazir. "After that, we can enjoy ourselves."

When he caught her dark gaze, Amritzar felt a pleasant surge of warmth in his belly. His wife really was very beautiful. She followed Islamic practice—she wore a head scarf and dressed modestly when she went out—but in the evening would dress up for her husband. Tonight she was wearing a tight sweater, a wide belt, and high boots. She had made up her mouth with special care and brushed mascara onto her long lashes.

"A phone call?" she asked in surprise. "Here?"

If it had been on his cell, she would have understood. But a call on the room telephone of a hotel they had just checked in to and which they would leave the next morning?

"That's right," said Amritzar, without explanation. When Benazir looked puzzled, he went over and put his arm around her waist.

"It's men's business," he assured her. "Afterward, I'll be all yours."

The young woman relaxed in his arms.

"I hope you'll give me a child," she murmured.

Benazir loved her husband as much as he loved her. He was a handsome man, with classic Middle Eastern looks, very dark eyes, and a strong nose and jaw. He spoiled her and showered her with love. A perfect husband.

Their lips were about to touch when the telephone rang, startling them both.

He ran to the phone and picked it up.

"Parviz?" asked an unknown man. The sound sent Amritzar's pulse racing.

"That's r-right," he stammered.

"I'm downstairs at the bar."

Amritzar had no time to say anything else. The man had already hung up.

"Wait for me here," he told Benazir. "This won't take long. You can watch television."

He was already at the door, feeling as moved as the day he had asked for her hand in marriage.

The hotel's lobby was as impersonal as its rooms, and the bar at the end of the hall was almost empty.

Sitting at a table was a swarthy man of about forty wearing a windbreaker over a heavy brown sweater. He didn't stand when Amritzar came over.

For a few seconds, the two men looked each other over, their absorption only interrupted when the bartender asked for their order. Without consulting Amritzar, the stranger ordered two Coke Zeros.

When they were alone again, the stranger extended his hand and quietly said in Urdu:

"Call me Mahmud, brother."

Feeling ill at ease, Amritzar sat down. The two men had communicated by email, but this was the first time they were meeting in person.

Mahmud broke the silence.

"I bring you greetings from those you sent your messages to," he said quietly. "They want you to know they are praying to Allah and his prophet Muhammad, blessed be his name, that your project prove successful, inshallah."

"Inshallah," said Amritzar.

In the presence of this confident stranger who represented people fighting for the faith and the triumph of Allah, Amritzar suddenly felt himself moving from dream to reality.

Six months earlier, he had learned that a missile from an American drone had killed his uncle, his three brothers, their wives, and five of their children. They all lived in the village of Miramshar in the tribal area between Pakistan and Afghanistan. The official explanation? "Regrettable collateral damage due to incorrect targeting data."

The coalition authority wrote a letter of apology to the local government and offered to pay for the funerals.

But under Islamic law, the bodies had all been buried the very day of the attack, and anyone who accepted dollars from the infidels would have had his hand cut off. The village imam had assured everyone that all the martyred *shahids* would be under Allah's protection until the end of centuries of centuries.

And that jihad would continue until the death of the last infidel.

When Amritzar learned the terrible news, he was shattered. He had never been particularly religious, but now he spent hours in the Newark mosque, trying to speak to God.

The imam there told him that Allah had sent this trial to test his faith. Over time, Amritzar gradually emerged from his despair, and pain gave way to a burning desire for vengeance.

Turning to Wikipedia, he plunged into the study of armed drones. He learned that the ones flown over Afghanistan were piloted long-distance by operators at a base in Nevada. The operators put in eight hours a day, then calmly went home to their families, risking nothing more serious than an occasional upset stomach or head cold.

Amritzar initially considered taking revenge on the drone pilots, but they worked on a very secure military base. Besides, he didn't know which individual fired the missile that wiped out his family.

He began to visit a mosque close to his home more often. He had always been a believer, and never missed Friday prayers, but he rarely went during the week, preferring to pray at home or in his warehouse.

In addition to telling the imam, Amritzar started sharing his newfound hatred of Americans with some of the faithful. One of them suggested that he check out a website said to be closely connected with al-Qaeda that regularly called for jihad.

Without much optimism, Amritzar created a Hotmail account so as to communicate in the website chat room, choosing his first name as his username.

He posted several messages expressing his desire to participate in jihad but got no answer. Then ten days ago, he received a Hotmail message from someone in a cyber-cafe calling himself Mahmud632. Amritzar of course noted the year of the Prophet's death.

Mahmud congratulated Amritzar for his desire to make jihad and asked him a few personal questions. They chatted online, mainly about religious matters. Then Mahmud suggested they meet in person, at the Newark Liberty hotel on Friday at nine p.m. Amritzar decided to take his young wife along, as he sometimes did on a weekend.

Now he was face-to-face with the man himself.

Mahmud leaned over and again spoke quietly in Urdu.

"You don't know who I am, but I've read the messages that you posted on the website. I believe you are a good Muslim and that you want to take vengeance on the infidels. Have you decided on a plan?"

Surprised by the question, Amritzar was silent for a few moments. After studying Mahmud's eyes, he decided to trust him.

"Yes, I have," he whispered.

"What is it? Do you think that the faithful who are making jihad can help you?"

"Maybe."

Amritzar's thoughts were racing. For months he had

dwelled on revenge while feeling sure that he would never be able to get it. After all, he was just a small businessman, a rug merchant. He was wealthy enough, but he didn't have any contact with the people who carried out attacks. What little he knew he'd learned on the Internet or by reading specialized magazines. And now this man at the table was turning a dream into reality.

"What will you do to avenge your family?" asked Mahmud, sipping his Coke.

Amritzar hesitated to answer, and Mahmud pressed him.

"We are fighting for the triumph of the same God, brother," he said. "You have to trust me. As I said, I've come here especially to weigh what is in your heart. Your emails show a sincere desire for revenge, but we have to be careful. The infidels are powerful and very clever. If you really want to avenge your family, you must be ready to sacrifice your life. To become a martyr."

"I'm ready!" said Amritzar, surprised by the firmness of his own voice. A strange exaltation had come over him.

"So tell me what you have in mind."

At that, Amritzar began to speak in a quiet, almost inaudible voice. Leaning close, Mahmud listened tensely.

"I need to get an Igla-S," he said. "It's a sophisticated Russian surface-to-air missile."

Mahmud stared at him in astonishment.

"How do you know about those weapons?" he asked. "I thought you were in the carpet business."

"I am, but I've learned a lot from the Internet. The

Igla-S is the most effective weapon against a plane or helicopter currently available. The missile is 72 millimeters in diameter and five feet long. It's shoulder-fired and weighs less than thirty pounds. The warhead travels at 1,755 miles an hour and is effective to an altitude of 12,000 feet. Iglas have already brought down American planes in Iraq and in Serbia. In Chechnya, the *boiviki* rebels have used them to destroy Russian Mi-8 and Mi-16 helicopters."

Amritzar had recited his lesson without pause, and Mahmud listened carefully.

"Have you ever fired one?"

"No, of course not," Amritzar said with a rueful smile. "I've only seen them in pictures. But I know everything there is to know about them. Did you read about the jihadist in Morocco—may Allah protect him—who built a bomb using only information he got from the Internet? He could barely read and write but was guided by the hand of Allah. His bomb killed seventeen infidels in Marrakesh and spread terror among the unbelievers."

Mahmud knew the story and seemed impressed.

Amritzar waited, his eyes downcast.

"What exactly do you plan to do with this missile?" asked Mahmud. "Assuming you learn how to use it."

"Shoot down Air Force One, the American president's plane," said Amritzar calmly. "With him on board, of course."

Mahmud clearly hadn't expected this. He was silent for a moment and took another sip of Coke. When he spoke, his voice was serious.

"That's a wonderful project, brother, but extremely difficult to carry out. You must know that since the blessed day of September 11, 2001, we have never succeeded in striking the Americans on their home soil."

"I know how careful they are," said Amritzar. "But I have a plan to get around their precautions."

"What's that?"

"I can't tell you yet. You know our proverb: the man who knows nothing can say nothing. Do you think you can help me?"

Mahmud realized that he was dealing with neither a fool nor a dreamer. He had really only arranged this meeting to be on the safe side. Most would-be terrorists chickened out the moment you met them. This man was different, and the gleam of hatred in his dark eyes was real.

Just the same, he needed to push Amritzar a little harder.

"Do you realize what you're risking?" he asked. "You have a beautiful young wife."

Amritzar's head jerked up.

"How do you know that?"

Mahmud gave him a sharp look.

"We know many things about you," he said. "We must be very cautious. The Americans are powerful, and they pursue us relentlessly. You might be an undercover agent, trying to draw us into a trap and destroy our organization."

"I'm not an agent!" cried Amritzar.

Mahmud opened his windbreaker and lifted his brown sweater, revealing the automatic tucked in his belt.

"If I thought you were," he said quietly, "I would take you outside and shoot you."

Amritzar looked at him coldly.

"If I were an undercover agent, I would have arrested you by now. And you haven't answered my question," he continued. "Can you help me get a working Igla-S?"

Mahmud was silent for a few moments.

"That's a question I can't answer," he admitted. "I will pass on the request. Give me your cell phone number. It will make contacting you again easier."

Amritzar did so.

"I'll call to set up another meeting," said Mahmud. "And don't ever, ever mention your project on the Internet."

"Of course not!" snapped Amritzar, annoyed that he was being taken for an idiot.

The two men stood up and hugged briefly.

"Don't try to follow me," Mahmud whispered. "It would be dangerous for you."

Amritzar watched as Mahmud went out the revolving door. Then he put a five-dollar bill on the table and left the bar. He felt as if he were walking on air. What had started as a vague dream of vengeance was becoming concrete, turning into a real project.

When he opened the door to his room, Amritzar was still elated. And when he saw Benazir, he felt happier still.

She was lying on her side, so absorbed in watching television that she didn't even turn her head when he came in. For his part, Amritzar couldn't take his eyes off the curve of her hips in her tight pants. He felt as if all the excitement of his conversation with Mahmud had now rushed to his crotch.

When he stretched out next to his wife, she started.

"Oh, it's you!" she murmured.

"Who did you think it would be?" he growled. "You're a she-dog, who would let any man lie with you. Yet you swore before the imam to be faithful."

Benazir realized she had made a mistake. She turned around and gently touched her husband's crotch.

"I hope you get me pregnant tonight," she said. "I very much want to have a child."

Amritzar put his hand on her hip and pulled her close.

"So do I," he said.

Actually, this was a lie. At that particular moment, all he wanted was to take his young wife from behind, the way he used to when they were engaged. He had wanted to marry a virgin, and they both developed a taste for anal pleasures.

Benazir was now feverishly kicking off her boots and pulling down her trousers, leaving only a skimpy pair of panties that Amritzar promptly yanked off. He raised his hips to shed his jeans, revealing bulging red underpants.

Once freed, his cock sprang into the air.

"What a beautiful thing you have," she said admiringly. "So big and hard."

She hadn't yet brought herself to perform fellatio on him, as American women apparently did. In her eyes it was haram—forbidden. A man's penis was made to enter certain openings in a woman's body. Not her mouth.

"Come here," said Amritzar, pulling her over.

Benazir obediently lay down on her belly, hips slightly

raised, arms stretched out before her. Then she reached back to spread herself for him.

Kneeling behind her, Amritzar pushed her thighs farther apart with his knee.

Trembling, Benazir gave a small cry when he entered her. It always hurt a little at the beginning, though she was dripping wet in front. Amritzar thrust hard, plunging deep into his wife's body. She gave a strangled shout.

"That's right!" she cried. "Deeper, darling."

Amritzar was now thrusting with all his might. Before his staring eyes floated the image of an Igla missile, as slim as a needle—which is what the word meant in Russian—and as deadly as a poison dart.

Plastered against Benazir's rump, he stopped for a few seconds to thank Allah for giving him so many joys in one day.

Panting, Benazir interrupted his brief pause.

"Don't come yet," she begged. "When you've enjoyed me, make me pregnant."

Amritzar was chatting with one of his customers, a wholesaler from Minneapolis, when his cell phone rang. It displayed no number. When he answered, he heard a man's voice.

"I'll meet you at the northwest corner of Forty-Second Street and Broadway at nine o'clock tonight." It was Mahmud, who immediately hung up.

It had been two weeks since their meeting, and Amritzar had given up hope of hearing from him again.

He found it hard to resume his conversation with the Minneapolis businessman. All he could think of was to go to his back office, unfold his prayer rug, and thank Allah for helping him with his revenge.

As he touched his forehead to the rug, it occurred to him that happy events never come alone. The previous night, Benazir had announced that she was pregnant. So he would be leaving a son behind if his project unfolded as planned. All of Miramshar would celebrate his exploit, and his widow would raise the child to honor his father.

At this point he couldn't be sure it would be a boy, of course, but he had prayed so hard, Allah could hardly refuse his wish to be a *shahid* who died fighting the infidel. The dearest fate for a believer.

Amritzar hoped the next few hours would pass quickly. The fact of the meeting meant that Mahmud had found a way to get the thing Amritzar most wanted: an Igla-S surface-to-air missile.

CHAPTER

2

A light rain was falling on Times Square, and the wind along Forty-Second Street drove the hurrying pedestrians to hug the walls of the buildings. Without telling his wife, Parviz Amritzar had taken the train in from New Jersey. Now chilled to the bone, he almost didn't recognize Mahmud, who was standing with his hands stuffed in the pockets of a hooded parka.

"We can't stay here," Amritzar said, as a blast of wind hit them.

"No," said Mahmud. "Let's go to the Sofitel bar."

The hotel wasn't too far away, and it was usually crowded, so they wouldn't attract attention.

Grateful for the warmth of the hotel lobby, they headed for the bar. They had to wait for a table; a lot of people seemed to have had the same idea, and come in from the cold.

Amritzar ordered coffee, and Mahmud, tea.

The two men looked each other over. Seeing Amritzar's eager expression, Mahmud said quietly:

"I think we'll be able to help you."

Amritzar silently thanked Allah. He felt he was moving into a different life. Though now on tenterhooks, he had to wait for their drinks to be brought before starting the real conversation.

Mahmud leaned close and spoke into his ear.

"I think we can find you an Igla-S, though it won't be easy. It's very hard to get hold of one."

"But many countries bought them from Russia, and from the Soviet Union before that," objected Amritzar. "Thousands of them."

Mahmud was unmoved.

"The people who acquired Iglas guard them carefully, and nobody else has access to them."

"So how would you manage it?"

"We have our sources," said Mahmud. "Many Iglas were stolen in Libya, and the thieves sold some of them to our friends. But it's going to take a while to get one into the United States. It would have to come by ship; in a container of fruit, for example."

"I understand," said Amritzar, "but I don't need one here."

Mahmud looked at him, baffled.

"Now I can tell you the truth, brother," Amritzar continued. "Until I was sure I could get a missile, I felt it was best that you not know the whole story. Since our last meeting, I've done a lot of research and have come up with a better way to strike than I first imagined. Look at this."

Amritzar took a press clipping from his pocket and handed it to Mahmud, who read it quickly. It was a short article from the *Washington Post* announcing that President Barack Obama would be making an official visit to Moscow the following month.

"You want to launch the attack in Moscow?" Mahmud asked in disbelief, handing the clipping back.

"Yes."

"Why? It just increases the risks."

"I know Russia a little," Amritzar explained. "I travel there occasionally to buy Caucasian carpets. Security measures in Russia are much less strict than in the United States. I also know that many jihadists have made their way to Moscow from the North Caucasus. Last year, two women from Dagestan blew themselves up in the Moscow subway. They belonged to Jamaat Ismail, a Wahhabi movement that fights for God."

Mahmud seemed stunned. When he was finally able to speak, he said:

"It's going to be very hard to get an Igla into Russia."

Amritzar dismissed the concern.

"It's not that big a problem," he said. "The missiles are manufactured there, and everybody knows that some Russian soldiers make money by selling military matériel to rebels in the Caucasus, even though the equipment might be used against them. I've read that Russian helicopters had been shot down by surface-to-air missiles that the Russians themselves sold to the Chechen *boiviki*. I'm sure you know our brothers there, so we ought to be able to get some missiles. Besides, I only need one."

Mahmud gaped at him, now completely at a loss. Finally, he said:

"Even assuming we could get you a missile, what would you do, all alone? You don't have any training."

"I've learned all the technical steps by heart," said Amritzar. "It's very simple; everything's on the Internet. I've memorized the whole manual. Besides, our brothers in Chechnya or Dagestan will help me."

Amritzar fell silent and sipped his coffee. Around them, couples were drinking, chatting, and flirting. Mahmud shot a contemptuous look at their cocktails.

"Look at those dogs, degrading themselves."

Amritzar stayed focused on his idea. Now that he'd glimpsed a successful outcome to his project, he wasn't going to let it go.

"Do you think you'll be able to help me?" he asked.

Mahmud slowly shook his head.

"I don't know. I'll have to ask. What you're asking is extremely difficult."

"Why?" asked Amritzar with feigned innocence. "The Iglas are manufactured in Russia. It must be easier to get some there than to bring one to the United States."

While logical, the argument didn't seem to appeal to Mahmud.

"I'll have to talk to the brothers about this," he said, gulping the rest of his tea. "This is a big operation, and it's going to cost a lot of money. An Igla-S sells for more than one hundred thousand dollars, and we'll probably have to pay more."

"The ones that were stolen in Libya didn't cost anything," Amritzar pointed out. "If our brothers have them, that should make things much easier."

Mahmud didn't answer. The Moscow angle of Amritzar's project had clearly taken him aback.

"I will be in touch," he said.

"I'm about to travel to Vienna to buy carpets," said Amritzar. "I'll be at the Hotel Zipser next week; it's where I always stay. After that I expect to go to Russia to buy Caucasian carpets."

"Do you already have a visa?"

"Yes."

Many Americans traveled to Russia these days, as tourists. There was nothing unusual in that. A naturalized U.S. citizen for the past seven years, Amritzar took advantage of it.

Amritzar let Mahmud exit the Sofitel first. He felt less intimidated by the al-Qaeda man than at their last meeting, and Amritzar knew he'd piqued his interest. That wasn't surprising. Al-Qaeda hadn't launched any big operations since Osama bin Laden's death. Marginalized in Afghanistan and Iraq, it was active only in politically turbulent Yemen. To reclaim its past glory, it absolutely had to launch another dramatic attack. Amritzar's project, even if it was difficult to execute, would be a spectacular way for the movement to take center stage again.

Amritzar ordered another cup of coffee. He didn't feel like going home yet.

He might be experiencing his last hours of real peace, he knew. His project, which once seemed insane, was beginning to feel achievable.

He had read a great deal about the fundamentalist Islamic uprisings in the Caucasus, an area where people were deeply religious and hated the Russians. Moscow had imposed on Chechnya a brutal leader named Ramzan Kadyrov. He claimed to be religious but battled the *boiviki* rebels who wanted to create an Islamic state. To help exterminate those who wanted to break away from Russia, Moscow was flooding the country with rubles. Fortunately, a few Islamist and Wahhabi groups were still active in neighboring Dagestan, where the population was even more religious.

Eventually Amritzar got to his feet. Leaving the bar, he saw that the rain had stopped, and he could walk to the subway. He wondered if he should take Benazir to Vienna with him, as he sometimes did. Particularly since her pregnancy would soon prevent her from traveling.

If he got a favorable answer from Mahmud before returning home from Vienna, he would travel on to Moscow.

Vengeance would take absolute priority in Amritzar's life, particularly now that he could see a way of accomplishing it. At times, a little voice would tell him that he might die in the attempt, but that was an abstract fear and he didn't give it much weight.

A chill wind hit him as he left the Sofitel. He walked quickly to the subway station at the downtown end of Times Square, and eventually rode back to New Jersey on the PATH train.

He prayed that Mahmud would send him news quickly.

———

Bruce Chanooz showed his I.D. card to the guard at the lobby of the grim high-rise in Alexandria. The Federal Bureau of Investigation occupied the entire twenty-three-story building. Chanooz tried to look self-possessed while waiting for his escort up to the counterterrorism center. This was the young agent's first visit to the holy of holies, and he felt intimidated.

Chanooz was assigned to the New York field office and rarely went out of state, and then only to New Jersey. He had come down to Washington by train—the most practical way to make the trip—and got off at Union Station.

A serious-looking female agent emerged from the elevator and asked him to follow her. FBI personnel assigned to other offices weren't allowed to move about the building by themselves.

Security here was an absolute priority, almost an obsession. Gray hallways, doors with access codes changing weekly, and an almost artificial atmosphere.

The two agents got off at the sixteenth floor, and Chanooz was led to an empty waiting room with curtained windows.

The silence was total. And yet the floor housing the counterterrorism center hummed with activity. This was where all investigations against individuals who might threaten United States security were coordinated. In cooperation with the Department of Homeland Security, the FBI had exclusive jurisdiction over the fight against terrorism on American soil, whether Islamic or domestic. The CIA wasn't allowed to operate within the

United States. In fact, if the agency suspected a traitor in its ranks—which sometimes happened, unfortunately—it was required to call the FBI in to investigate.

This was humiliating, since the two federal agencies cordially despised each other.

The door was opened by a man who looked like a younger version of Groucho Marx. He had large, yellow-tinted glasses, a huge mustache, and a shock of black hair.

When he stretched out a hand, he gave Chanooz a dazzling smile, something not often seen among the buttoned-down FBI agents.

"I'm Assistant Director Leslie Bryant," he said. "As you may have heard, I head the division you work for."

Bryant ushered Chanooz into his nearly empty office and waved him to a seat across from his desk. Manners here were formal, but Bryant grinned again when he said:

"I hear you've been doing good work, 'Mahmud.'"

CHAPTER 3

Bruce Chanooz looked down modestly.

"Thank you, sir. Just doing my job."

The young special agent had been working for the FBI for only three years. Normally, he would have paid his dues doing scut work, but he had a skill that was invaluable to the bureau. His Pakistani father, a fabric importer in Los Angeles, had immigrated to the United States thirty years earlier, and the family spoke only Urdu at home, while using English outside.

As a result, Chanooz was perfectly bilingual in Urdu and English.

And ideal for the FBI's Vanguard program.

This was a secret program that nobody outside the bureau knew existed. A few highly placed members in the White House and Washington political circles suspected, but were careful not to say so.

In fact the Vanguard program was the cutting edge of America's fight against terrorism. Since the September 11 attack, the United States had become paranoid. More than anything, the country feared a repeat of the attack

on the World Trade Center, which had deeply traumatized the nation.

Increasingly drastic measures had been taken, evolv-
ing to meet the changing threats. Security checks spread
at airports. Colored alerts were displayed at each United
States border crossing, signaling the terror threat level. It
was always red.

The problem was that the federal agencies charged
with counterterrorism—the FBI, CIA, NSA, and the
Department of Homeland Security—were doing such an
effective job that there hadn't been any more terrorist
attacks on United States soil.

Just the same, the war on terror remained the key-
stone of White House policy, and a frightened public's
main demand. It was certainly the only point on which
Republicans and Democrats agreed. To most people, the
fact that months and even years had passed without any
arrests of terrorists suggested that the fight was lessening.

That was actually far from the truth.

So at the highest levels of the FBI, the Vanguard plan
was born.

It was perfectly simple.

The FBI collaborated on counterterrorism with the
National Security Agency, which handled electronic surveillance. Using its sophisticated technology, the NSA
was able to penetrate Islamist sites and retrieve messages
sent and received.

From time to time it also learned the identity of
American citizens who corresponded with these inflam-
matory sites.

Some were hotheads, who expressed deep hatred for America.

That wasn't against the law, as freedom of speech is a sacred pillar of American democracy. You can express all sorts of opinions on the Web, even the most outrageous ones. Insulting the president of the United States is no crime. But some of the website visitors—fanatics with no connection with al-Qaeda or other terrorist organizations—went further.

Loners would proclaim their desire to wage international jihad, even if they were pizza deliverymen or unemployed drifters in a distant corner of the Midwest. Some wrote to Islamist sites to ask for instructions on building homemade bombs, for example. Others frankly stated their desire to attack the United States.

Naturally, the Islamist sites never answered them, out of caution.

Thanks to the NSA, from time to time the FBI would get names of Americans proclaiming evil intentions. The bureau could then send an undercover agent pretending to be an envoy from those sites, to see how dangerous the people were.

Of course, the FBI would immediately identify and track them, using phone taps and surveillance to see if any steps had been taken to put the plans into effect.

Which was never the case.

Most of the people were amateurs, unconnected with any subversive organization, with neither financial means nor know-how. When questioned, they quickly abandoned their fantasies and quit dreaming.

But every so often the FBI would identify a more persistent individual who had developed an actual plan of attack. This is how the bureau discovered a naturalized American of Lebanese descent named Ryan Moussaoui who was bitterly angry at the United States over massacres in Iraq.

He had written an Islamist site with a specific project: to park a car bomb in Times Square and blow it up when two nearby movie theaters let out. Moussaoui was a car mechanic who worked in the Bronx. He was married and had two daughters, no criminal record, and no connection with any terrorist groups. That was why he was asking for help from anyone who could help with his project.

The FBI had weighed the measures to be taken.

The easiest would be simply to arrest and indict him, but the bureau lawyers put the kibosh on that. An FBI charge unsupported by evidence of specific steps to execute the project wouldn't survive five minutes before a judge. Having bad intentions isn't illegal. You can get drunk and loudly announce on the Net that you plan to blow up the Statue of Liberty to avenge Afghan children, and it's no crime.

But Moussaoui's plan was very specific, and the FBI wanted to find out if he had any accomplices. The division in charge of analyzing threats decided to contact him. But not in the usual way, which would consist of sending a pair of special agents to apprehend the suspect.

Instead, Moussaoui received an email sent from a cybercafe. It was from a certain Amin who claimed to be part of the Salafist movement and congratulated Moussaoui on his courageous statement.

Moussaoui answered, and the two men began to exchange messages about their shared hatred of America. But they remained relatively cautious, aware that email is easy to intercept.

One day Amin suggested that they meet. He set the rendezvous in an out-of-the-way part of Brooklyn, in a neighborhood of African immigrants.

Amin had dark skin and a short beard and wore work clothes. He seemed intelligent and knew all about jihad.

Moussaoui was impressed to meet a man who seemed to have connections with the world of jihadists. But he had to admit to Amin that his plan for an attack hadn't taken concrete shape. Thanks to the Internet, he had a pretty good idea of how to make a car bomb, but he didn't have a vehicle or explosives, or the means to buy them.

Moussaoui went back to his job without having gotten anything concrete from Amin. He had no idea what he had set in motion at FBI headquarters in Washington. Leslie Bryant, the assistant director of the counterterrorism center, consulted a FBI legal advisor about his plan, to make sure he was acting within the law. The answer was clear: If you can produce in court recordings of your conversations with the suspect that showed his intent to commit a federal crime, said the lawyer, your action is legal.

Reassured, Bryant launched the Vanguard program.

Results had exceeded all expectations. From Amin, Moussaoui received the money to buy a vehicle: an old Jeep Wagoneer, paid for in cash. Amin gave him explosives and two gas cylinders, and even helped install the explosive device in the vehicle. On the chosen day, Moussaoui parked the Wagoneer next to the two Times Square cinemas, started the timer, and ran away.

He didn't get far. He was almost immediately captured by a team of FBI agents, and charged with launching a terrorist attack. He didn't know that the detonators furnished by Amin had been duds.

When Moussaoui was tried in Brooklyn in Federal Court, his lawyer argued that the attack hadn't been real, since all the elements of the crime had been furnished by an undercover FBI agent. The jury decided he was a potentially dangerous individual, even though he had been helped in his deadly project. Moussaoui was sentenced to forty-seven years in prison, without the possibility of parole.

After the verdict, the FBI had been mobbed by reporters. The press was full of praise for the bureau, which was apparently able to unmask the most secretive of terrorists.

The Vanguard plan was successfully off the ground.

A year later, Fox News was still stressing the terrorist threat.

Leslie Bryant, the assistant FBI director in charge of the Vanguard program, smiled warmly at the man opposite him and opened the file on his desk.

"Special Agent Chanooz," he said, "I've carefully studied the file on your new operation. I think it has real possibilities. What do you think of this man Parviz Amritzar?"

"He was traumatized by the deaths in his family," said Chanooz. "He's developed a deep hatred for our country, which he holds responsible for these deaths, whether true or not."

It was likely to be true, since only the Americans used armed drones in the area.

"How far along is he in his project?"

"For the moment it's just theory. He doesn't have any concrete elements, except a fairly comprehensive knowledge of how to handle an Igla-S surface-to-air missile."

The official leaned forward eagerly and said:

"Can you confirm what's in your report, Bruce? That this individual plans to shoot down Air Force One, killing the president of the United States?"

"That's correct, sir. He told me that in several of our conversations."

"And you were able to record these conversations? Can they be played for a grand jury or a district attorney?"

"I think so, yes, sir," said Chanooz.

The assistant director leaned back with a slight smile.

"In that case, congratulations on your good work. Since this Parviz Amritzar needs an Igla-S missile, we're going to help him find one."

Colonel Sergei Tretyakov carefully reread the confidential message he'd just received from the FBI office in Moscow, which was housed in the American embassy near the Garden Ring road.

It was signed "Bruce Hathaway, Operations Director, Federal Bureau of Investigation, Moscow," which suggested involvement at the highest levels of the bureau. The document bore a rectangular red *Top Secret* stamp at its upper left corner. Torn by mixed feelings, the colonel gazed out the window at the dark sky over Lubyanka Square.

Times certainly had changed.

Now working with the FSB—Russia's domestic intelligence service—Tretyakov was a veteran of the KGB's First Directorate, the aristocracy of Russian intelligence until Boris Yeltsin dissolved it in 1991. Tretyakov had been stationed abroad several times, including London and Amsterdam. In those days, the KGB's dealings with the Americans were hard-fought and hostile. When he came back to Moscow, Tretyakov had enthusiastically joined the war against undercover CIA agents in Moscow who were trying to recruit sources.

They rarely succeeded, usually being arrested along with their contacts by agents of the Second Directorate, the KGB's counterintelligence arm. They were hauled down to the Bolshaya Lubyanka, where the process was always the same. The CIA agents were interrogated, and then released and deported, because they had diplomatic immunity. Their Russian recruits, on the other hand, were sent to Lefortovo prison. Once their confessions were obtained by the appropriate methods, they were tried, sentenced, and shot, either in a Lefortovo inner courtyard or the third subbasement of the Bolshaya Lubyanka building. This was now the FSB's headquarters, and the building where Colonel Tretyakov had his office. The change of roles had created some lingering bitterness.

For example, a member of Tretyakov's graduating class had been shot for accepting a fistful of dollars from the Americans. The man worked in the same department he did, and the betrayal derailed Tretyakov's career. He had been shunted off to the Second Directorate, where he would have no contact with foreigners. People didn't fool around with traitors in those days.

And now the American Federal Bureau of Investigation was officially asking Tretyakov to give it an Igla-S, Russia's technologically most advanced surface-to-air missile, for an antiterrorist operation.

It gave him heartburn.

The building housing the FSB offices rose like a black slab near the top of Bolshaya Lubyanka Street, and still struck terror in the hearts of those who knew it in an earlier era. But it wasn't the same.

Lubyanka Square had lost the gigantic statue of Felix Dzerzhinsky in August 1991, when the new president ordered it taken down. The former KGB headquarters across the way, an impressive brick building with rows of windows, today housed inoffensive bureaucrats instead of the powerful secret service chief. Executions were no longer carried out in the Lubyanka basement, and the KGB existed only in memory.

But thanks to Vladimir Putin's efforts, vertical power had returned to the security services under a new set of initials.

Run directly by the Kremlin, the FSB now controlled all of Russia. Intelligence operatives—the *siloviki*—had achieved the KGB's impossible dream: becoming the country's real rulers, without oversight from the once-powerful Communist Party. Provincial governors were named by the Kremlin, not elected. And FSB agents kept tabs on the population as efficiently as their predecessors in the old KGB Second Directorate had.

But a quasi-democratic façade hid this cold and efficient ferocity. More than anything, Russia was concerned about its international reputation. Which was why the FBI and the FSB had signed an agreement in 2003 to cooperate in the fight against terror. This was a common interest, as the Kremlin was seriously alarmed by separatist movements in the Caucasus, which were led by Islamists or Wahhabists, often financed by Saudi Arabia.

Under Putin's iron hand, the problem was being contained. Chechnya had been turned over to the pro-Russian tyrant Ramzan Kadyrov, and Dagestan brought off with billions of rubles.

Contacts between the FSB and the FBI or CIA were now handled by the Fifth Directorate, which was in charge of information and international relations.

Colonel Tretyakov stamped the American document to show that he had read the request, put it in an envelope, and sealed it. Then he called his secretary, who appeared a few moments later.

Anna Polikovska was a good-looking woman of about forty, the daughter of a military intelligence officer who had died of cancer. She was haughty, with a striking, slightly angular face, and full breasts emphasized by tight sweaters. Like many Russian women at this time of year, she wore a heavy sweater, a tight skirt slit up the back almost to her thighs, and very high-heeled boots.

"Take this to the 'czar,'" said Tretyakov with a smile, "and then make me a cup of tea."

Anna took the envelope and left the office, followed by the eyes of her boss, who enjoyed looking at her ass. Anna intimidated him a little, otherwise he would have long since tumbled her on a corner of his desk. He knew little about her life except that she was divorced and almost certainly had lovers.

She drove a little French Peugeot 207, which she parked on the first garage basement level among the FSB's higher echelons' Mercedes and Audis.

Anna's FSB salary was decent, but it couldn't have paid for the full-pelt mink coat with the animals' little tails that she wore. And Tretyakov viewed the fact that she wore black stockings every day as evidence of loose morals.

Alexander Bortnikov, the head of the FSB, learned of the American agency's request the next day, and it struck him as odd. He immediately wrote back to Tretyakov, asking him to call in an FBI representative to ask for more information.

He then photocopied the document, stored the original in his office safe, and put the copy in an envelope under a wax seal with his name and rank.

The orderly who guarded his hallway office popped in within seconds of being summoned. It was as if he slept beside Bortnikov's door, though it was armored and protected by a sophisticated electronic system.

The FSB chief handed him the sealed envelope.

"Take this to Rem Tolkachev's office in Korpus Fourteen."

"Right away, sir."

Korpus No. 14 was the Kremlin's operations building, a few blocks away. You took Okhotny Ryad and Manege Square, then turned left into Red Square. A pedestrian entry to the Kremlin stood beyond Lenin's mausoleum.

As it always did in November, an oppressive, dark gray sky covered Moscow like the lid of a pressure cooker.

Malko Linge glanced at his fiancée, who was spreading her day's purchases on their bed at the Sacher. Alexandra was wearing lace Dior panties so expensive, they must have been woven by fairies, smoky-gray stockings, and high heels that emphasized her long legs.

As always, she was an incredible turn-on. The young woman seemed to float in a cloud of come-hither desire.

Malko told himself he would have to wait until after their evening to enjoy her—as he always did—but he was itching to get his hands on her now.

Alexandra turned around, holding a chiffon Valentino dress against her body. It was as black as sin and sheer enough to invite trouble.

"Do you like it? Shall I wear it tonight?"

Malko looked at his watch.

"I'll let you decide," he said. "I have a meeting downstairs in a few minutes."

Alexandra's beautiful mouth widened in a sarcastic smile.

"One of your spooks?"

"Who greatly admires you," he said. "He would probably prefer meeting you than me."

Though sorely tempted to help her into the Valentino dress and then tear her panties off, Malko got out of his chair to leave. Despite all the affairs he had during his assignments, he remained deeply attached to Alexandra and lusted for her as intensely as he had at twenty.

Down on the ground floor he walked into the Rote Café. Its red-velvet walls had long welcomed everybody who was anybody in Vienna for lunches and dinners.

There were only two people there. One was an old Viennese man absorbed in reading the *Wiener Beobachter*, a local rag that covered society events. The other was a tall, gray-haired man in an elegant, slightly old-fashioned three-piece suit. He was drinking a beer. This was Jim Woolsey, the Vienna CIA station chief. A charming man, Woolsey had been assigned to the Austrian capital six months earlier and taken the trouble to call on Malko at Liezen Castle, where he'd caught a glance of Alexandra.

Woolsey was one of Malko's espionage contacts, the people who allowed him to live according to his station without stooping to reprehensible activities. What the CIA asked of him was often completely illegal, but it was for the right cause. If he ever had a truly serious problem, he would wind up not in jail but in Arlington National Cemetery, buried among the other foreigners who'd given their lives for the United States.

"*Wie gehts?*" asked Woolsey, who was making an effort to learn German.

"*Sehr gut,*" answered Malko, before shifting to English. Woolsey's German was still a work in progress, and nowhere near as good as Secretary John Kerry's fluent, if accented, French.

The waiter offered them a choice of two brands of vodka: Russky Standart and Beluga. Malko went with the Beluga, whose almost unreal silkiness belied its 42 percent alcohol content.

"You're lucky I'm here in Vienna for an evening event," he said. "Otherwise you'd have to drive out to Liezen."

All too aware of bugs, the two men used the telephone only for inconsequential chitchat.

"I'm guessing you have an important request for me," Malko continued. "Like heading for some godforsaken corner of the world where one bad season is followed by an even worse one."

"No, no, nothing like that!" said Woolsey, raising his hands in mock alarm. "It's just a little thing. You won't even have to leave Vienna."

Malko distrusted "little things," which often grew into big ones—dangerous, apocalyptic problems.

"I'm all ears, but please make it short," he said. "Alexandra's coming down as soon as she's ready."

"I'll be delighted to say hello to her," said Woolsey, his eyes a bit moist. He lowered his voice. "It involves some information about the bureau."

CIA people so disliked the FBI, they tried not to even use its name. The agency people considered their bureau counterparts to be regulation-obsessed morons who approached intelligence work with out-of-date methods and an endless fascination with minutiae.

Malko was intrigued. How could it concern Vienna?

"Is this coming from Washington?" he asked.

"No, Moscow."

"Really?"

"That's right. The bureau has a major office there, and it cooperates with the FSB on certain matters."

"Intelligence?"

"No, terrorism, something the Russians are very nervous about. They're scared to death of the Salafists and al-Qaeda. All the problems they've had in the last years have come from the crazy Muslims in the Caucasus who combine Islam with separatism. They've carried out lots of attacks in Moscow, and they're still doing it."

"I know," said Malko. "I was in Moscow in 1999 when the Chechens blew up four buildings and killed two hundred ninety-three people."

"Well, the Caucasians are still at it," said Woolsey darkly. "Ten months ago a guy from Dagestan blew himself up at Domodedovo Airport."

"What's the connection with the FBI?" asked Malko, aware that time was passing.

Woolsey dropped his voice even further.

"It's top secret," he said. "You know that we're especially concerned by electronic espionage in Moscow, where the Russians are experts. The Cold War isn't quite over, even if we pretend otherwise.

"Here's what happened: one of our bug teams was sweeping a local CIA office, and we accidentally came across an internal FBI document."

Without showing it, Malko smiled to himself at the word "accidentally."

"What was it?"

"An email from FBI headquarters in Washington to their Moscow office. It said that the New York FBI office had turned up a Pakistani-born naturalized American terrorist named Parviz Amritzar. He's a New Jersey rug merchant, and he's planning an attack that the bureau wants to stop by infiltrating his network."

"Is he planning to blow up the Brooklyn Bridge?" asked Malko sarcastically.

"No. He wants to use a surface-to-air missile to shoot down Air Force One with the president aboard."

"That's a lot more serious! So what now?"

Jim Woolsey looked around, then said:

"He wants to use a Russian Igla-S for the attack."

"That's strange! Why?"

"We don't really know. He apparently considers the Igla the most reliable missile out there."

"And is it?"

"Just about," said Woolsey. "We did some research, and it turns out the Igla-S is probably the best at overcoming electronic countermeasures."

"So how does this involve me?" asked Malko, taking a sip of his Beluga.

"Langley ran Amritzar's name through the computer, but nothing came up. Then we spotted it on some websites connected to al-Qaeda—actual terrorist sites—and on emails to those sites. Amritzar wasn't offering information; he was asking for help."

A hush descended on the two men.

"Are you saying that this Amritzar person isn't connected to a terrorist group?" asked Malko.

"Not as far as we know."

"In other words, the FBI is taking someone with bad intentions and turning him into a full-blown terrorist."

"That's what we're afraid of," said the CIA station chief. "They've done it before. The bureau only cares about results."

"So where does the agency come in?"

"Well, the bureau people don't know the Russians as well as we do. They've gone and asked the FSB to lend them a working Igla-S, never imagining that the Russians will turn around and screw them."

Malko took it from there.

"Let me guess," he said. "An FBI agent pretending to be an arms dealer will bring Amritzar a missile. At that point the bureau will sweep in and arrest him."

"That's about it," said Woolsey. "But Langley isn't absolutely positive Amritzar *isn't* connected to a terrorist group. Which might be the case, even if they can't get him a missile. We'd like to know for sure that he's clean before he gets in too deep with the bureau."

Malko finished his vodka, aware that Alexandra could walk in at any moment.

"So how can I help you?"

"Amritzar will be in Vienna in two days. As I said, he sells carpets. Apparently he's here to buy some. We'd like you to make sure that he doesn't have any suspicious contacts during the two days he plans to be here. I know this isn't normally up your alley, but Ted Boteler in operations is asking it as a favor."

It certainly wasn't what Malko was expecting. And he had no intention of doing the stakeout himself. His faithful butler and bodyguard, Elko Krisantem, could handle that perfectly well.

"I'm always glad to help Ted," he said. "Give me the details."

"Amritzar will arrive Thursday morning. He's staying at the Hotel Zipser, at 49 Lange Gasse in the Josefstadt neighborhood."

"Do you have a photo of him?"

"We don't, and we'd like to have some."

"That can be done. Do you have any idea what he looks like physically?"

"No, but he's traveling with his wife. She's also Pakistani and apparently very beautiful."

"That's not exactly a description, but I think we can figure it out. Tell you what: I'll bring you my report and the photos at the embassy on Monday." He smiled. "Along with a list of any terrorists he meets."

Woolsey smiled in turn.

"I suspect it'll be a very short one."

Just then, Alexandra came into the café, her sable coat open over the Valentino dress. Jim Woolsey leaped to his feet as if the U.S. president had entered the room.

When she stopped at their table, his gaze surreptitiously moved to her neckline. The black chiffon was cleverly cut to reveal most of her breasts.

"*Shatzi*," said Malko, "do you remember Jim Woolsey?"

Glancing at the paralyzed American, she said:

"No. Should I?"

Malko thought Woolsey was going to melt like a snowball in a fire. He quickly softened his fiancée's remark.

"There were a lot of people at Liezen that day."

Some color returned to Woolsey's face.

By then Malko was on his feet. Alexandra gave Woolsey a haughty nod and strode toward the exit. Malko turned around and quietly repeated:

"You'll get everything on Monday."

Parviz Amritzar was closing up shop earlier than usual—he was due to fly to Vienna that evening—when the doorbell rang. He turned, about to tell the man that he was closing, when he recognized Mahmud.

He came closer and whispered:

"Can we go into the back office?"

Feeling rattled, Amritzar led him to the small, glassed-in office.

"What are you—" he began.

Without answering, Mahmud took a thick envelope from his inside jacket pocket and set it on the desk.

"There's two hundred thousand dollars in there," he announced. "The brothers have decided to help you. In Moscow you'll meet a man who will sell you an Igla-S."

"But I'm going to Vienna first."

"No problem. Just keep checking your email. As soon as things are ready in Moscow, you'll get the green light." Mahmud was already heading for the exit. "And be careful with that money; it's precious."

The door slammed before Amritzar could recover from his surprise. With trembling fingers, he slipped the rubber band off the envelope. When he saw the wads of hundred-dollar bills, he felt dizzy.

His jihad had begun.

General Andrei Kostina put the note from Alex-ander Bortnikov with the attached FBI request on his desk and looked at it with disdain.

Kostina didn't like Americans and he didn't like Jews, considering them equally responsible for the collapse of the Soviet Union. Naturally, his main hatred was aimed at Mikhail Gorbachev, "the man with the birthmark," who had allowed it all to happen. The idea of helping the Americans made Kostina sick. And yet it made sense for the FSB to turn to him, the deputy director of Rosoboronexport.

The FSB didn't have any Igla-S missiles. It could get one, but jumping through the bureaucratic hoops would be slow and complicated. Russian army units certainly had stocks, and each unit had an all-powerful FSB political commissar. But commanders protected their assets jealously, and could be hard to budge.

Only Rosoboronexport, the Russian military export agency, could easily get hold of the missiles.

Kostina turned to his computer to see if any Igla-S

were readily available. They were manufactured at Izhevsk in the Urals for regular Russian army use and for export. He learned that twelve hundred were being assembled, a batch that was ordered and partly paid for by Indonesia, but the Izhevsk factory was behind schedule. The only entity that could quickly supply a few would be the surface-to-air missile research center at Kolomna, a town about seventy miles southeast of Moscow on the M5 highway to Chelyabinsk.

Kostina noted all this in the document's margin, and added his opinion that it would be risky to put a working Igla-S in American hands. The missile was already six or seven years old, but the United States might not have discovered all its secrets.

In short, the general would have vetoed the proposal if it were up to him, but his opinion was only advisory. He put the paperwork in an envelope and called for his secretary. He would pass the buck to the GRU, Russia's military intelligence agency.

"Take all this to General Shliaktin," he said.

The GRU chief ruled from the "Aquarium," a group of large white buildings off Polezhaevskaya Chaussée in the Khoroshevskiy neighborhood. Hidden among tall apartment buildings, the GRU headquarters featured dozens of ultramodern security cameras, razor wire, an impressive black front gate that was always closed, and a helicopter landing pad on the roof.

The agency's basic outlook hadn't changed with the end of the Soviet Union. It remained steeped in a culture of secrecy, rabid nationalism, and a visceral distrust of anything American.

As the head of the GRU, General Alexander Shliaktin's opinion was much more than advisory. He alone would decide whether to accede to the FBI's request or to bury it in a diplomatic refusal.

Since seven o'clock that morning, Elko Krisantem had been sitting behind the wheel of the old orange Opel he usually drove on errands for Liezen Castle. The car was parked near the Hotel Zipser, a modest four-story building in the center of Vienna.

Despite having gotten up at five to sit in the damp cold, Krisantem was happy to be there. The previous evening, when Malko explained the assignment, he was delighted. He might be only a devoted butler now, but Krisantem had once been a killer for hire in Istanbul. The old Turk still occasionally joined Malko on missions as a bodyguard or even an assistant, but that happened less and less often.

While looking after Liezen Castle, he periodically oiled his old Parabellum Astra, and in his pocket he kept the cord he once used to strangle bad guys.

Krisantem rubbed his chilled hands together. To save gas, he had turned off the Opel's motor. Anyway, in this quiet Vienna neighborhood nobody would notice the old car parked across from the Zipser.

Suddenly he jerked upright in his seat. A taxi had just

stopped in front of the hotel, and a woman was getting out. Ensconced in a fur coat that fell to her ankles, she wore very high-heeled boots and a fur hat. She was followed by a dark-skinned man who looked Middle Eastern. The cabbie took a suitcase out of the trunk, and the couple entered the hotel.

It was 8:25 a.m., and the odds were good that this was Parviz Amritzar and his wife.

Krisantem waited for a while, but the two didn't come back out. So he took his cell phone, rang the hotel, and asked to speak to Herr Amritzar.

After a brief pause, the operator said:

"I'll connect you now."

Krisantem immediately hung up and phoned Malko.

"They have arrived, Your Highness. What would you like me to do?"

"Stay close to them," he said. "And take some pictures as soon as you can."

As he did every morning, Rem Tolkachev got to his Korpus No. 14 office in the south wing of the Kremlin early. Protected by a sophisticated electronic access code, his door displayed no sign, but all the Kremlin orderlies—the "gray men"—knew their way to it.

Nobody knew how long Tolkachev had been there; it seemed to be forever. In fact, he had served every Russian leader from Gorbachev to Putin.

Raised in Sverdlovsk, Tolkachev was a born *silovik*, humorless and incorruptible. Whenever a new "czar" came to power, Tolkachev would have a brief conversation with his new superior and be reconfirmed in his position.

In the Kremlin, Tolkachev's mission was simple: solve problems that were difficult or impossible to undertake officially.

His office safe held all the buried secrets from the tumultuous transition that followed the collapse of the USSR.

Tolkachev's methods hadn't changed over the decades. Several times a week, he would be consulted on some burning issue. He would usually come up with a solution and immediately communicate it to the current president by internal Kremlin messenger. His proposal would come back, either approved or denied.

It was rarely denied.

The president would also sometimes ask him to solve a problem himself, giving him the latitude to do whatever he thought necessary.

Most of the orders Tolkachev gave were oral. If a written instruction was necessary, he typed it himself on an old Remington, in a single copy. He distrusted electronic communications.

Finally, every head of the various security agencies, whether civilian or military, was aware of Tolkachev's position and knew he was to be obeyed without question.

Rem Tolkachev was the czar's armed right-hand man.

The little white-haired gentleman drove a gleaming Lada through the Kremlin's Borovitsky gate every morning and parked in the area reserved for the highest apparatchiks.

He'd been a widower for the past decade. He had lunch every day at the Kremlin's Buffet Number 1, where you could get an excellent meal for less than 120 rubles. In the evening he did a little cooking in his apartment on Kastanaevskaya Street in western Moscow.

Tolkachev had hardly any social life. He had no friends, and only a few people who dealt with him professionally even knew what he looked like. All they knew of him was a somewhat high-pitched voice with a central Russian accent.

The rare visitors to his office left unimpressed. The walls were bare except for a calendar, a picture of the current president, and a poster of Felix Dzerzhinsky, the creator of the Cheka, published on his death in 1926.

Tolkachev served his visitors only tea, which he himself drank very sweet.

In the reinforced cabinet at the back of his office, Tolkachev kept files on all the people he had used in the course of his long career. There was a little of everything: crooks, swindlers, killers, priests, former security agents. . . .

To manipulate these helpers, Tolkachev had unlimited supplies of cash. When he ran low, he would write a note to the Kremlin administrator, and the money would be brought to him the same day. No accounting was required. Everybody knew that Tolkachev was compulsively honest. In the days when they were still in circulation, he wouldn't pocket so much as a kopeck. His only pleasure was to serve the *rodina*—the nation—and its incarnation, the current president.

In fact, his role was enormous. Behind the surface of what looked like a nation of laws, Russia swarmed with parallel legal services, clandestine little offices ready to do anything to help the Kremlin. Tolkachev enforced iron discipline to keep these often unruly people in line.

Today he opened the first file on his desk and lit one of the slim, pastel-colored cigarettes that he smoked when he wanted to think.

The file had been brought from the office of Alexander Bortnikov, the head of the FSB, the night before.

Tolkachev studied it carefully, made some phone calls to check his options, and smoked a few more cigarettes. Then he turned to his Remington and, with two fingers, started typing.

The short memo—Putin hated anything longer than fifteen lines—read:

"I propose trapping the Moscow FBI chief and charging him with military espionage so we can exchange him for Viktor Bout, who is currently in prison in the United States."

Tolkachev needed the president's assent before launching such an operation.

Five minutes later, a man in gray was at his door. Tolkachev opened the automatic lock and silently handed him the sealed envelope addressed to the president of the Russian Federation.

He knew he would get a quick answer.

Krisantem was glad the day was nearly over. All he'd had to eat since this morning was a *doner kebab* gulped down while his target had a long meeting with a Caucasian and Pakistani carpet wholesaler.

The Amritzars had emerged from the hotel around eleven and taken a taxi on Operngasse. They strolled around the majestic Staatsoperbuilding, then had lunch in a pizzeria.

The woman was dressed the same way as the previous evening. When she took off her coat, Krisantem saw that she had a slim figure, an attractive face, and a mouth whose bright red lipstick contrasted with her modest head covering.

The couple had then split up. He took one taxi, and she, another.

Women rarely played an active role in the Muslim world, so Krisantem elected to follow Amritzar, whose taxi took him to the carpet dealer. Through the window, Krisantem could see Amritzar in conversation with a fat, friendly looking man with a mustache. The men were seated in the showroom and were examining carpets. It was an ordinary business transaction, and it gave Krisantem a chance to get a bite to eat.

Night was falling when Amritzar came out of the showroom. A radio taxi came to pick him up and bring him to the Zipser.

From which he had just emerged with his wife, once again walking toward the opera. Like good tourists, they settled on the Hotel Sacher terrace, which gave Krisantem a chance to take a few photos.

Deep down, the Turk felt he was wasting his time. Amritzar's activities seemed perfectly innocuous.

Nothing about him spelled terrorist.

But he was conscientious and decided to stick with the couple until they returned to the hotel for the night.

The request sent to Putin came back just when Tolkachev was preparing to leave his office for a performance at the Bolshoi. The show started at eight, but with traffic, you had to leave extra time. He preferred to drive, though he could have requested one of the Kremlin's limousines. These were black Audis with tinted windows, a police light on the left side of the roof, and a special siren whose distinctive blasts chased other vehicles out of the way.

In a holdover from Soviet days, a central lane in the major avenues was reserved for special vehicles to use as they pleased. For a small fortune, a few oligarchs had been assigned the necessary permit, knowing that the *politsiya*—the heirs of the old Soviet *militsiya*—would never stop them.

Tolkachev opened the envelope. It contained his memo with a single word written in the left-hand margin: "*Da.*" Seeing that gave him deep satisfaction. He knew he was just a high-grade functionary, but the idea that he shared Vladimir Putin's views was intoxicating.

He had thought of Viktor Bout because neither the FSB nor the Kremlin's diplomatic efforts had been able to stop the arms merchant's extradition to the United States. A diplomatic defeat.

Bout was hardly an exalted personage, just a former GRU agent gone rogue. But he had remained faithful to his country. He had never betrayed Russia, and had provided the secret services with valuable information. He had behaved well and confessed nothing.

Above all, he was Russian.

So he had to be freed.

Tolkachev was happy to help gain Bout's eventual release, even if it was mainly a matter of national pride.

What he now had to figure out was how to lure the head of the Moscow FBI into a trap.

From his desk, Tolkachev picked up his ticket to the Bolshoi. The great opera house had just opened after years of renovation, and he was excited to see it in its new skin.

He would deal with the FBI matter tomorrow. He just had to devise the trap.

Anna Polikovska was sitting at a table in the mezzanine of the Chokolade Mitza on Baumanskaya Street. From her vantage point, she could watch the stairs leading up from the main room. The cup of tea before her was empty, and the café nearly so. There were just a couple of women chatting and two men watching the flat-screen TV. But Russians love chocolate, and in an hour the place would be jammed.

Suddenly Anna started: a man was climbing the stairs. Unfortunately, it wasn't her lover, Alexei Somov. It was a fat, bald man who looked at her suggestively, probably taking her for a prostitute. Anna was wearing black stockings, a tight sweater, and high-heeled boots. Moreover, she was elegant, carefully made up, and alone. To avoid appearing provocative, she deliberately looked away.

Somov was late, as usual, which is why they always arranged to meet in public places.

Anna called the waitress over and ordered a cup of chocolate.

That was a mistake.

The chocolate arrived just as Somov's bearlike figure appeared on the stairs, and Anna felt a wave of warmth in her crotch. When he reached the top, her thighs parted of their own accord, restrained only by her tight skirt. Somov stirred her sexually in a way no other man ever had.

Physically, he was an animal. He stood six feet five, and everything about him was big, from a pair of massive hands to a jaw like a hungry lion's.

Grinning, Somov plopped into a chair next to Anna and automatically put his hand on her black-clad thigh.

"You're looking very pretty, *zaika maya*," he said, watching his "bunny's" nipples stiffen under the sweater as he casually brushed against them.

The waitress came over to their table.

"What would you like, sir?"

Anna answered for him: "The check, please."

Somov grinned, his almond-shaped eyes twinkling.

"You in a hurry?" he asked playfully.

Anna shot him a look that would give a dead man a hard-on. In a husky voice, she said:

"Yes, I am."

She was already on her feet, taking her mink coat from the rack. Somov helped her into it, his touch on her shoulders enough to give her goose bumps.

Anna went downstairs first. Somov's black Mercedes with the tinted windows was parked at the corner. She slipped inside and he joined her.

"I'm taking you to the GK tonight," he said. "A very good pianist is playing there."

Anna looked at him steadily.

"Afterward," she said.

Somov got the point, and they headed directly to the Metropol instead. These days, only certain Russians used the old hotel, where Somov had a permanent reservation. The annual room rent was paid by some mysterious organization or other.

As Somov drove, Anna announced:

"I have a little surprise for you."

"What's that?"

Without answering, she took his right hand and set it on her thigh while shifting in her seat to free her skirt. Somov's huge fingers slid up her stockings until they encountered naked skin . . . and something else.

"*Bozhe moy!*"—my God!

Somov's hand had just encountered a garter belt. Feeling unexpectedly stirred, he gripped Anna's thigh. She smiled.

"When I left the office, I did a little shopping at ZUM," she said. "You always told me that garter belts turned you on. I slipped into this one in the Mitza ladies' room . . . for you."

Somov's interest in the GK restaurant now vanished completely. It took them less than five minutes to get to the Metropol. Inside, Anna proudly led the way, the mink tails on her coat swaying. In the elevator she pressed herself against Somov, squeezing his cock through his pants.

Then she stuck her slender tongue in his mouth while he played with her breasts.

But when he moved down to her crotch, Anna moaned and said:

"No! Wait!"

She was too excited, on the verge of coming at the slightest caress.

Somov's room was at the end of the long hallway, and she practically ran down it. The room was dusty and ill lit, but it had a huge bed, six feet wide.

In seconds, Anna was undressing her lover. Every time she saw his powerful chest, huge thighs, and the bulge in his underwear, she melted.

Laughing, Somov stretched out on the bed and slowly slid his briefs down, revealing a thick cock, as upright as a ship's mast. Staring at it, mesmerized, she reached behind her back to unzip her skirt, and stepped out of it.

Then Somov saw the black belt and garters holding up Anna's stockings.

"Why, you dirty little slut!" he cried delightedly.

Anna jumped onto the bed without bothering to remove her coat or boots. First she stretched out next to her lover, rubbing against him like a cat. Then she straddled him, raising herself far enough to place the stiff cock between her legs. Her hand was barely big enough to go around it.

"You're something else tonight!" she muttered.

Her face tense and chest upright, she pushed her

panties aside with her right hand while firmly grasping Somov's cock with her left. When she felt the swollen glans against her, she sighed and lowered herself onto it, biting her lip. For a moment nothing happened. She was incredibly excited, but her labia wouldn't stretch far enough to admit the huge thing.

Fortunately, Somov was as excited as she was. He put his huge hands on her hips and pulled her downward. There was a kind of jerk, and he sank in an inch or so.

"Stop!" she cried. "You're too big!"

She might as well have been talking to an icon on the wall. Somov simply pulled her down harder. Unresisting, Anna was open-mouthed, in pain, and happy.

He raised her up again, only to penetrate her even deeper. She was as tight as a virgin, and the sensation was so delicious, he could hardly stand it. Gradually, natural lubrication took over, and the huge cock slid easily. Anna began to ride him furiously, hissing like a steam engine. Slipping his huge hands under her, he grabbed her ass, giving her yet another spasm of pleasure.

"Oh, God," she moaned. "I love it when you hold me like that."

Shoving her bra aside, she played with her nipples while Somov rhythmically raised and lowered her, each time going deeper.

As he penetrated her as far as he could go, Anna suddenly cried out, then collapsed on top of him.

Somov, who hadn't come, rolled away from her, then grabbed her hips and forced her to kneel on the bed. In the armoire mirror, the sight of the woman bent over, rump high and thighs stark white against the black garters, nearly drove him crazy.

When Anna felt the thick cock slamming into her from behind, she shouted and immediately started coming again. This triggered Somov's own orgasm, and he crushed her under his weight.

After a long moment, Anna spoke up.

"Let's go to the restaurant. I'm starving. We can come back here later."

The GK pianist was playing Italian tunes to an almost empty dining room. Anna had slipped off one of her high heels and was using her right foot to stroke her lover's crotch opposite her. The restaurant was dark, and anyway, nobody watched the customers too carefully.

A waiter arrived with a crystal bowl full of caviar—Beluga, smuggled from Kazakhstan. It had been a long time since you could get real caviar in Russia; it was all farmed but still cost 8,000 rubles a serving.

A delighted Anna started eating it by the spoonful, like an old Russian boyar. Money was never a problem with Somov. After leaving the GRU, he'd gone into black-market arms sales, specializing in bypassing Rosoboronexport and selling weapons to embargoed countries.

Anna couldn't describe exactly what Somov did, except that he traveled a lot, abroad and to the Caucasus, which had a flourishing arms market. Russian soldiers' pay was low and vodka expensive, so the troops often sold their equipment to their separatist Islamist opponents, at the risk of being killed with it.

"Stop that," hissed Somov. "You're gonna make me mess up my pants."

Using her toes almost like a hand, Anna seemed to be trying to make him come.

"Can't you wait a little?" he asked.

She quit fooling around and said:

"I just remembered something I wanted to tell you. You'd never believe it, but the Americans want to borrow an Igla-S from us."

She told him about the FBI's request and the response from the FSB. Somov stopped eating the caviar. His brain cells were starting to fire, a Pavlovian response to the word "Igla."

His Islamist customers in Dagestan had been asking for surface-to-air missiles for months. They weren't the nicest of people, needless to say: a separatist Wahhabi group, though secretly supported by Dagestan president Astanov.

The Igla-S was the best surface-to-air missile on the market, but very hard to get hold of because Russia only sold them to a few trustworthy countries. However, Somov had learned that one unit had sold some to Chechen *boiviki*, who used them to shoot down Russian helicopters.

Naturally, that was a bit messy.

He also knew that people under Wahla Arsaiev—the most important Wahhabi separatist leader in the Caucasus—were prepared to pay a million dollars for a missile, though its list price was just $180,000. Dagestan was rich. The little country on the Caspian had a population of only two million, but Vladimir Putin gave it two billion dollars every year, to keep it quiet and within the Russian orbit. The money was distributed by Astanov, mainly to his relatives.

Besides Caucasians, Somov's customers included Syrians, Armenians, several African countries, and in general anybody who wanted to buy weapons and had the means to pay for them but couldn't acquire them on the open market—like Colombia's FARC guerrillas.

Of course he couldn't carry on such delicate work in Russia without an influential protector. Somov's *kricha* was General Anatoly Razgonov, currently the GRU's number three man, and a veteran of black ops and the Caucasus.

The arrangement between the two men was simple. Somov would strike a deal only after getting approval from Razgonov. In return, the general supplied Somov with the weapons he needed. Payments were made in Luxembourg to offshore accounts that Razgonov managed. Thanks to generous commissions on the arms sales, plus the fees earned on these outside funds, both parties profited. The GRU officers got secret funds to draw on, and Somov got a life of luxury.

Anna's Igla-S story now gave Somov an idea. It would have golden possibilities, provided he could put together a somewhat tricky operation. It would be like the old days, like the time the Ministry of Defense sold Syria 150 brand-new T-72 tanks in 1995. They were carried on the army's books as having been destroyed by Chechen *boi-viki*. In fact, their paint hadn't even been scratched.

Anna withdrew her foot and slipped her shoe back on. With a questioning look at her lover, she said:

"Shall we?"

She was clearly eager for a rematch.

Somov dropped a fistful of five-thousand-ruble notes on the table and followed her out. This is really a red-letter day, he thought to himself. Not only was he going to fuck a woman wearing porn-star stockings, but she might have put him onto a very lucrative deal.

7

Bruce Hathaway's black Chevrolet stopped in front of 4 Bolshaya Lubyanka, but he told the driver to park a little farther up the gently rising street. Hathaway, the head of the FBI office in Moscow, was feeling tense. That morning, Colonel Tretyakov of the FSB's Fifth Directorate had sent word that he wanted to see him at two thirty.

The Fifth handled international relations, so this had to be the answer to Hathaway's request for an Igla-S to bait the trap the bureau was setting for Parviz Amritzar. If it worked, the Pakistani American would be facing decades in jail.

Unless the Russians said *nyet*.

Hathaway glanced up at the dark façade of FSB headquarters, which reminded him of the ominous black monolith in the film *2001: A Space Odyssey*. This was the seat of power in Russia, the place where the Kremlin's darker schemes were put into effect.

Entering the tiled lobby, he was promptly accosted by a guard in a gray uniform.

"May I help you, sir?"

"I have an appointment with Colonel Sergei Tretyakov," he said in passable Russian.

The guard led him to the front desk, where his passport was taken and the colonel's office called. A few moments later, a receptionist announced blandly:

"Colonel Tretyakov is expecting you. You'll be escorted upstairs."

Hathaway was given a visitor's badge and asked to follow an officer in a gray uniform who moved as smoothly as a robot.

On the eighth-floor landing, an attractive secretary awaited him. She was wearing a long straight skirt, high-heeled boots, and a gray sweater that matched her eyes. She waved him toward an open office door.

"Good morning, Gospodin Hathaway. I'm Anna. Please come in."

Colonel Tretyakov was in civilian clothes. A short, stocky man with an expressionless face, he slowly got up and came over to shake hands with his much taller visitor. The two men sat on a red Chesterfield sofa, and the secretary appeared carrying a tea tray.

"Chai?" asked the colonel, who didn't offer any other choice.

"*Da, pozhaluista*," said Hathaway. He remained silent while the colonel filled two cups with very hot tea, Russian style.

Tretyakov then got to the point.

"We have studied your request, Gospodin Hathaway," he said in excellent English. "After consulting with the appropriate authorities, Director Bortnikov has decided to grant it. We are deeply committed to the fight against terrorism."

"We appreciate that," said the FBI official warmly. Hathaway had come up with the idea of asking for a missile and was so pleased, he could have hugged the little colonel.

"We are happy to apply the terms of the 2003 accords," said Tretyakov in the same monotone, as if to give himself cover.

Hathaway could hardly sit still.

"When do you think we can get what we asked for, Colonel?"

Tretyakov remained impassive.

"Very soon, but there is a technical problem. We can't put our hands on an Igla-S right away. They are all assigned to military units, and the Izhevsk factory is on a tight schedule fulfilling an order from a foreign country. We will therefore use our Kolomna research center, which can produce the missiles in small batches."

"Thank you very much," said Hathaway, who knew exactly what the colonel was talking about.

For his part, Tretyakov was aware that the Americans knew all about Igla-S manufacturing; he wasn't giving any secrets away.

Glancing ostentatiously at his watch, he wrapped up the meeting.

"There you have it, Mr. Hathaway. I will contact you as soon as we have solved this little problem, and our two services will set up the operation."

He was already on his feet. The two men shook hands.

Once outside, the American briskly strode the hundred yards to his Chevrolet. Bolshaya Lubyanka was one of the few streets in Moscow where parking regulations were enforced. One of the others was Petrovka Street, where *politsiya* headquarters was located at number 38.

Hathaway was eager to share his good news, but he refrained from phoning his office, knowing the call would be monitored. But once in the embassy, he ran to his deputy Jack Salmon's office. He found him reading *Sports Illustrated*, which had just arrived in the diplomatic pouch.

"We're in, Jack!" said Hathaway. "The Russians have agreed. We're going to screw that damned Pakistani."

Salmon jumped up and gave his boss a high five.

"Well done!"

The two men did a little jig that is nowhere described in the FBI training manual. Then Hathaway came down to earth.

"Where is our actor now?" he asked, reverting to bureau-speak.

"He's in Vienna, buying carpets. We can contact him through Mahmud's cybercafe to get him to come here."

"Go ahead," said Hathaway. "I'll update Washington by email. But we'll have to bring Mahmud to Moscow."

"Not necessarily," said Salmon. "We're introducing Amritzar to a new 'terrorist,' so we don't have to give the guy a legend. He's supposed to be an arms dealer, so he could be Russian or Caucasian. Let me see who's available in-house. I think Soloway could play the part."

"Have Amritzar tell Mahmud what hotel he's staying at here," said Hathaway as he left.

Once in his own office, he switched on his secure computer and treated himself to a cigarette. Smoking was forbidden, of course, but this was a big day.

Leslie Bryant, head of the FBI's Vanguard program, could have kissed his computer screen when he saw Hathaway's email appear.

The bureau was going to catch a terrorist in the act, and do it with the help of its longtime enemy, the Russian FSB. A real coup.

Bryant would cast it as a textbook case of effective collaboration, and it might well give his career a boost. This was the best day of his life since the death of Osama bin Laden.

He picked up the telephone.

"Get me Special Agent Chanooz right away, please."

He would have to stay on top of this, he knew. But he could already see the front pages of the newspapers, announcing this extraordinary success.

Amritzar read the message that had just arrived from the now-familiar Hotmail address: "Go on to Moscow. Things look good. Give me the name of the hotel where you will be staying. Mahmud."

Thrilled, Amritzar gazed at the message. He'd been

right to persist. His dream was getting closer. He would become famous and avenge his family. He hadn't met his local contacts in Moscow yet, but he was sure that they would help him.

He also didn't know where in Russia Air Force One would be landing, and he still had to work out the logistics. But if these people could get him an Igla-S, they could certainly help him with those details. After all, he and the Caucasus Wahhabists had a common enemy, the United States of America.

Benazir gave her husband an intrigued look.

"Good news?" she asked.

"Yes," he said with a smile. "I got an interesting bid for a batch of Caucasian carpets in Moscow. I think we're going there before heading home."

The young woman glowed with pleasure.

"That's wonderful! I've always dreamed of going to Russia. Do you suppose we can sample their caviar?"

"I'm sure we can." He had gotten Benazir a visa at the Russian consulate in New York, just in case.

Suddenly Amritzar realized how desirable his wife was. He stood up and took her in his arms. She relaxed, and pressed her crotch against his.

"Hold on a moment," he said. "I have to change our plane tickets. I hope we can get a flight."

He phoned the hotel concierge and asked him to make them reservations on the first flight to Moscow tomorrow. When he hung up, he saw Benazir gazing lovingly at him.

They were already on the bed and in each other's arms when the telephone rang: they were booked on an Aeroflot flight the next day at noon.

Amritzar immediately sent an email to Mahmud:

"I will be at the Hotel Belgrade on Smolenskaya Street tomorrow."

When he got back into bed and Benazir started stroking his chest, Amritzar had the feeling that Allah was kissing his soul.

While her husband was on the phone, the young woman had quietly slipped off her panties, and Amritzar penetrated her almost immediately. He made love to her with even more passion than usual, while trying to ignore an unpleasant little thought: that becoming a *shahid* often involved a one-way ticket to paradise.

Despite the sun, dense fog lingered over the airport at Schwechat, east of Vienna. Malko parked his Jaguar in the garage and walked into the terminal. Thanks to Elko Krisantem's diligent surveillance, he knew that the Amritzars had a reservation on an Aeroflot flight at twelve.

Two hours earlier, the old Turk had watched the couple load their luggage in a taxi for the airport. He waited a few moments, then ran into the hotel, holding a package.

"Is Herr Amritzar still here?" he cried. "I have a delivery for him."

"I'm afraid he just left," said the desk clerk with an apologetic smile. "He's taking a noon flight for Moscow. I made the reservation myself."

Krisantem was already out the door. He took a moment to phone Malko at Liezen Castle, then headed for the airport.

By the time Malko entered the terminal, the Turk was behind a column near the Aeroflot ticket counter, discreetly taking pictures of Amritzar and his wife as they stood in line.

This was the first time Malko got to see the couple in the flesh. The woman in her head scarf was very pretty, he noticed. Bundled in a blue parka, Amritzar looked like what he was, an ordinary businessman.

Malko had encountered plenty of terrorists in his life, and he didn't sense that Amritzar was a veteran of the clandestine life. As the CIA suspected, he might have bad intentions, but he felt like a naïf.

Malko and Krisantem hovered nearby for half an hour, until the couple headed for the boarding gate.

"Did you notice anything special, Elko?" asked Malko. "Did he meet anyone?"

"No, they just went shopping. He visited a carpet dealer twice, but that's it. I don't know if they got any calls, of course, but no visitors."

"I think we've wasted our time. Since I'm in Vienna, I'll take the pictures and my report to the embassy and tell them we've drawn a blank."

That way, at least he would be finished with this boring chore.

The Jaguar in the embassy courtyard drew admiring glances, as did Malko's photos of the Amritzars spread out on Jim Woolsey's desk.

"I can't thank you enough," said the station chief. "Langley makes some odd requests sometimes. Your surveillance confirms what we already thought, that the FBI is creating a terrorist out of whole cloth."

"They have to justify their existence somehow," said Malko. "And Amritzar certainly does hate the United States."

"Well, he has his reasons. If a missile wiped out your family, you'd react the same way."

"Probably," said Malko. "Okay, I'm heading back to Liezen now."

"Please give my regards to Alexandra," said Woolsey, in a tone of admiration. "You're lucky to know such a beautiful woman."

No sign indicated the entrance to Military Hospital Number 7, which was used for funerals. It was located down a little side street in the Lefortovo neighborhood.

When he arrived, Alexei Somov bought a bouquet of red carnations from the florist's cart in the courtyard. Some fifty people were there, stamping their feet in the cold. He spotted the tall figure of Anatoly Razgonov near the entrance. The general was wearing a gray leather coat that reached his ankles, and a gray hat that just barely covered his bald head.

They were there for the funeral of a GRU officer named Anatoly Shlykov. A superb intelligence analyst, Shlykov had revolutionized Russian military doctrine by pointing out the general staff's strategic errors, and had been awarded the Order of the Red Star. He had been one of the most astute students of the USSR's enemies.

The crowd began to move as people lined up to pass by the coffin, and Somov slipped behind Razgonov. While waiting to enter the crypt, the two men exchanged a complicit smile. Somov had come to the ceremony knowing that his *kricha* was sure to be there.

It allowed him to meet with Razgonov discreetly without going to the Aquarium, where his visit would be registered. This was important, because the operation he had in mind was blacker than black. It had to be executed in complete secrecy, unconnected to an official agency like the GRU.

He was sure that Razgonov would appreciate his discretion.

Standing one behind the other, the two men made their way into the room next door. It was very cold and smelled of incense. An honor guard of four uniformed GRU soldiers in *shapkas* stood like wax statues by the coffin, their eyes vacant. As was traditional, the top of the coffin was open, and family members gathered around: a somber-looking man and a blond woman—Shlykov's widow—her head covered with a black mantilla and her eyes red from weeping.

Flagstaffs displayed the standards of the regiments in which the dead officer had served. There was neither music nor religious symbols.

Somov laid his carnations on the coffin and mixed with the crowd.

General Razgonov went to stand next to the coffin and, as a respectful hush fell, began his tribute to the dead man.

"*Tovarich offizier . . .*"

Everyone present had been cast in the same Soviet mold, and speech habits die hard.

As soldiers carried armfuls of carnations to the hearse that would take Shlykov to the cemetery, Somov and Razgonov slipped away.

Somov caught up with the general and quietly asked:

"Do you have time for lunch?"

When Razgonov hesitated, Somov pressed him:

"I have something interesting I'd like to discuss with you."

The two had known each other since the days when Razgonov was the head of military intelligence in the North Caucasus region, which included Chechnya, Ingushetia, and Dagestan. At the time, Somov commanded a special FSB unit whose task was to set local Caucasian groups against one another. Its methods were often questionable, but they were effective.

It was also in charge of targeted killings. When Somov's men kidnapped a *boivik*, he would disappear forever, thanks to the "pulverization" method he'd perfected. The prisoner was tied to an artillery shell that was then exploded, leaving no trace. When they were feeling humane, the soldiers first shot the victim in the back of the head.

For his black operations, Somov got the weapons he needed from Razgonov, who was still a colonel then.

Over time, the two men became friends and eventually started selling weapons to customers who had no right to have them, at astronomical prices. In the Caucasus, everybody had money. The only trick was to avoid counterfeit currency.

When they returned to Moscow, they continued their operation, which benefited both Somov and the GRU.

Somov now anxiously awaited the answer to his invitation.

"All right, but it'll have to be quick," said Razgonov. "I have a two o'clock meeting. There's a little Azeri restaurant near the Lefortovo prison. We'll take my car."

The two men were finishing a delicious kebab lunch. The restaurant's customers were locals, and nobody would ever imagine that one of the most powerful men in Russia was sitting in a booth in the back.

"So what did you want to tell me?" asked Razgonov, sipping his tea.

"You know that business of the Americans who want to borrow an Igla-S from us, right?"

Razgonov frowned.

"How do you know about that?"

Somov smiled.

"I was very well trained, *tovarich* general."

"Why does it interest you?"

"Igla-S are very hard to get," said Somov. "And I know people who are prepared to pay ten times the list price for one."

"What people?"

"Nobody you'd want to see socially: the Wahla Arsaiev group."

"You're crazy, Alexei Ivanovich!" snapped Razgonov, shaking his head. "We can't do that. Those people are enemies of Russia."

Somov smiled slightly.

"You're aware that three of our Mi-8 helicopters were brought down by Igla-S in Chechnya, right? They were sold by a colonel we both know, who needed money for his mistress."

"He deserved to be shot," said the general angrily. "I've never betrayed the *rodina*, and I'm not about to start now."

"Neither have I," said Somov smoothly. "I'm not suggesting betrayal, just putting some money in your coffers by piggybacking on the Americans' plan, without any danger for Russia.

"You can release a small number of Iglas on your own authority, and I have buyers for them. After that it gets trickier, but it's safe. I still have a lot of rich friends in Dagestan."

Somov explained his scheme at length, but Razgonov remained dubious.

"You realize that if this doesn't work, I'd have to shoot myself," he said. "After having you executed."

"I know, but it will work," said Somov. "Think about it, and call me. We can have a drink at the Metropol. There are always pretty women there."

The general finished his tea and put on his long leather coat, leaving the four-thousand-ruble check for Somov to pay.

Razgonov said good-bye without indicating that he would follow up on the scheme, but the arms merchant was pretty sure he would.

"Can we get together quickly?" asked Jim Woolsey.

Malko was a little surprised. They'd just seen each other three days earlier.

"Is it urgent?" he asked. "I wasn't planning to come to Vienna."

"I can drive out," said the station chief. "I'd be delighted to see Liezen Castle again."

"All right," said Malko. "Come for tea this afternoon."

Which was just a manner of speaking, since neither man drank tea.

When he'd hung up, Malko went to find Alexandra. She and Ilse the cook were planning a dinner for the end of the week.

"We're having a visitor," Malko announced. "My friend Jim from the embassy."

Alexandra was wearing a black sweater and a pair of tight riding pants that were even more flattering than a skirt. The very picture of a sexy gentlewoman farmer.

"Do you want me to change and drive him really crazy?" she asked with a smirk. "Last time, he kept leering at me. I thought he wanted to jump me."

"I sometimes feel like jumping you, too."

Alexandra gave him a challenging look.

"You're not the only one."

Seated on a corner of the red-velvet sofa where Malko had often paid homage to Alexandra and various visiting girlfriends, Woolsey was finishing his coffee. Alexandra had gone to greet him, after changing her clothes. Woolsey had to struggle not to stare at her breasts, which were elegantly set off by a black Dior lace blouse.

"So what's going on?" asked Malko.

"We don't really know yet," said the American, "but a couple of warning lights are flashing. Remember the people you spent time tailing, the Amritzar couple?"

"I don't have Alzheimer's yet," said Malko with a grin. "That was three days ago. What's going on? Have they gone underground?"

"No, they're in Moscow, at the Hotel Belgrade."

"So what?"

"The FSB has formally asked us what we knew about them. Whether they have any connection with international terrorism."

"Is it usual for them to approach the agency this way?"

"It happens from time to time," said the CIA station chief. "A matter of mutual courtesy. We do the same thing. Only there's a hitch."

"What's that?"

"The Russians know perfectly well that Amritzar is being set up by the FBI and doesn't have any connection with any al-Qaeda movements."

"Maybe they just want to make sure."

"Yeah, maybe. . . ." Woolsey didn't seem convinced.

"So what did you tell them?"

"The truth. That the guy wasn't in our database, that as far as we knew he had never been in touch with any of the groups we're tracking."

"So what then?"

"They thanked us."

"They're careful."

"No, they're vicious," said Woolsey. "We've dealt with them long enough to know that. I'm wondering what they're up to. They don't do anything by accident."

"That may be true, but how can I help you?"

"Langley would like you to go to Moscow. You know the Amritzar couple, and you've had a lot of experience with the Russians. We can't ask the Moscow station to look into it. If there was ever a leak, the bureau people would be furious. Whereas if you show up as an observer on the lookout for dirty tricks, it would be different."

"Is it really important?" asked Malko.

"Yes, it is."

Woolsey was still smiling, but his eyes were cold.

"No one will know why you're there," he continued. "Maybe we'll just be treating you to a vacation."

Malko didn't believe a word of it. When the CIA asked him to go someplace, it was *never* for a vacation. Behind the American's bland reassurances, Malko could detect a whiff of death.

CHAPTER

8

Alexander Bortnikov was struggling to contain his impatience. The FSB director was sitting in his armored Audi, which was stopped in traffic behind an equally armored black SUV carrying his bodyguards.

It was only a fifteen-minute walk from FSB headquarters on Bolshaya Lubyanka to the Kremlin, but a man of Bortnikov's importance didn't walk. He had to be driven, and enter the Kremlin by the Borovitsky gate. That meant his car had to drive around Red Square, along Kremlevskaya Embankment, and up Borovitskaya Square. Only then could Bortnikov enter the holy of holies.

Unfortunately, a collision between a semi and a VW Golf had created a huge traffic jam near the Kremlin's red walls.

If you have an accident in Russia, you can't just exchange insurance information and go on your way. The *politsiya* has to write a report, even for a fender bender. And it takes the cops a long time to show up.

The driver of Bortnikov's Audi furiously sounded its special siren but was blocked by the mass of stopped cars.

Finally, they got under way and raced toward the Borovitsky gate. Alerted, the cops on duty switched all the stoplights to green.

The driver stopped in front of Korpus No. 14, and Bortnikov hurried inside to the elevator. It didn't do to keep a man as powerful as Rem Stalievitch Tolkachev waiting.

The old spymaster never called on people he wanted to see, except within the Kremlin itself.

Bortnikov pressed the buzzer and Tolkachev's office door immediately swung open. Seated behind his desk, the spymaster smilingly invited him to sit down.

"Greetings, Alexander Vladimirovich," he said. "I was afraid you weren't coming."

The squeaky voice put Bortnikov ill at ease, and the undisguised reproach made him feel like a little boy.

"You're aware of the American request for an Igla-S, aren't you?" Tolkachev continued.

"I am. I forwarded it to you."

"We have decided to respond favorably."

Bortnikov displayed no reaction, well aware that "we" meant the president.

"How would you like me to proceed?"

"There are two parts to this affair," said Tolkachev, scratching his neck. "The first consists of finding a working Igla-S for the Americans. The GRU will take care of that, so you don't need to be involved. Colonel Tretyakov and his people will handle the details.

"You, on the other hand, will deal with the most delicate part of the operation. We've decided to take this opportunity to charge one of the Moscow FBI agents with espionage."

Ah, back to the good old Soviet methods, thought Bortnikov. But then a doubt crossed his mind.

"How can we do that, Rem Stalievitch?" he asked. "We're the ones who are putting the missile at the Americans' disposal. This isn't a clandestine operation. No FSB agents have been approached."

"You don't know the whole story," said Tolkachev crisply. "The Americans have been lying to us. They claim to need the missile so they can charge an American citizen named Parviz Amritzar with terrorism. But we checked with the Central Intelligence Agency, and its Moscow representative Thomas Polgar says they know nothing about him. The CIA tracks terrorists very carefully; that's their job. Yet they've never heard of this man and haven't found anything linking him to terrorist organizations.

"We know that the Americans haven't learned all the Igla's secrets. So we find it suspicious that they would request a live, functioning missile. In this kind of operation, you would use a dummy. But because of the 2003 agreement, we can't turn down their request."

He fell silent.

Bortnikov understood that Tolkachev was giving him the official version of the operation, but it seemed pretty far-fetched. If the Americans wanted to get an Igla-S, it wouldn't be hard. There were plenty of them floating around Libya, and countries that needed money, like Greece, would be happy to sell one. But it wasn't Bortnikov's place to question state policy.

"What role will my agency play?" he asked.

"You will brief the counterespionage section about the attempt to penetrate our military," said Tolkachev. "They are to set up round-the-clock surveillance on all FBI agents. When one of them and the Pakistani meet with our agents to take delivery of the missile, your officers will arrest them both.

"Amritzar will be charged with arms trafficking and imprisoned in Lefortovo.

"Your men will take the FBI agent to your office for interrogation, then turn him over to the attorney general, who will have received his instructions. Once the charge has been formally made, he will be sent to Lefortovo prison pending trial."

Bortnikov mentally reviewed what he just heard, and raised an important point.

"CIA personnel assigned to Moscow have diplomatic immunity and can't be taken to court," he said. "We can only deport them. But that's not the case with FBI people."

"Exactly right," said Tolkachev approvingly. "I checked their status. FBI agents aren't allowed to conduct intelligence operations on Russian soil. Their activities are aboveboard, in liaison with your or some other Russian federal agency. So they don't have diplomatic immunity.

The operation will therefore have judicial consequences. Is all that clear?"

"Perfectly," said the GRU chief, getting to his feet. "I'll make the necessary arrangements."

Tolkachev looked at him sharply.

"Needless to say, this is a compartmentalized operation."

"Of course."

Bortnikov shook Tolkachev's parchment-dry fingers and made for the door, which opened before he touched it. Walking down the empty hallway, he felt cheerful. Happy days were here again.

The Kremlin obviously had something in mind, he thought. They wouldn't dream of hauling a Moscow FBI agent into court for something like this. The Americans would go to war over it.

So there was some other reason involved, but Bortnikov didn't need to know what it was.

Amritzar gazed out his hotel window at the looming bulk of the Ministry of Foreign Affairs a hundred yards away. It was one of the monstrous "wedding-cake" buildings put up in Stalin's time: massive blocks of architecture decorated with towers and thousands of windows.

The Hotel Belgrade itself had hardly changed since his last carpet-buying visit to Moscow. A great white slab, it displayed no indication that it was a hotel. Inside, the common areas were reduced to the strict minimum. It had a tiny lobby with a bar in the back. A red-carpeted hallway served the elevators, watched by a bored hotel staffer.

"Can we go out for a walk?" Benazir asked eagerly. By chance it wasn't too cold, and the beautiful blue sky seemed to have drifted in from another season.

"Later," promised Amritzar.

It felt odd to be there, planning an attack.

He turned on his computer and checked his email. One message jumped out at him:

"You will be contacted by a man named Yuri. You can trust him. Mahmud."

That must be the person who will get me an Igla-S, thought Amritzar. Al-Qaeda really was a powerful, far-flung organization.

Benazir was looking at the décor of their room, which was one of the Belgrade's renovated ones. It had a real double bed and cost 4,200 rubles a night, not including breakfast. The other rooms retained their depressing Soviet look: yellowing walls with narrow twin beds set head to foot. Very few foreigners stayed at the Belgrade; the guests were mostly Russians from out of town. But the hotel had its advantages: it was cheap and centrally located, right across from the Arbat, Moscow's famed pedestrian shopping arcade of boutiques and souvenir stores.

Amritzar was feeling at a loss. He didn't speak Russian and didn't know Moscow that well. Plus, he would need a car to get to the place where he would fire his missile.

The room phone suddenly rang, and he started. He

picked up the old Bakelite handset and heard a man's voice.

"Parviz Amritzar?"

"Yes."

"This is Yuri. I'm down in the lobby."

Heart pounding, Amritzar turned to his wife.

"I have a meeting downstairs. We'll go for a walk afterward."

In the lobby, he found a man sitting on a bench facing Smolenskaya Street. He had close-cropped hair and was wearing jeans and a padded leather jacket. He looked a little like the actor Daniel Craig.

"Parviz?" the man asked, getting up.

"Yes."

"I'm Yuri. Let's have a cup of coffee." He spoke good English.

They sat on stools at a high table across from the bar. A sexily dressed blond woman was seated at the next table. She was doing her nails and didn't glance at them.

After their coffee was brought, Amritzar asked the question that was on the tip of his tongue.

"Are you the person who . . . ?" he asked quietly.

"Yes, I am. But there's a hang-up. I don't have what we need yet. You'll have to wait a little while."

"How long?" asked Amritzar anxiously.

"Not long. Do you have the money?"

"Yes, I do. Two hundred thousand dollars." The cash that Mahmud gave Amritzar in New York, just before he left.

"Good."

Yuri looked at his watch and said:

"I'm going to give you the number of a Russian phone—mine. But you have to watch what you say. The FSB listens to everything."

"I'll need your help beforehand," said Amritzar quietly. "I have to scout the area."

"Where will that be?"

"I don't know yet. Can you find out which airport the U.S. president is coming to? I already know the date. Also, I need you to get me a car."

"We'll see about that," said Yuri evasively. "I just sell stuff, that's all."

"But you know people who can help me, right?"

"I'll see."

"Mahmud must have friends here," Amritzar said, lowering his voice even further.

Yuri didn't answer.

Amritzar realized that Yuri spoke English perfectly. He even had an American accent.

"Are you Russian?" he asked, intrigued. "You speak very good English."

The man looked at him sharply.

"I was born in Ingushetia, but I've lived in the United States. I'll call you when the time comes. Do you have a Russian cell phone?"

"No."

"Then I'll call the hotel."

"What about a car?"

"I'll let you know," said Yuri. He put a hundred-ruble bill on the table. The waiter gave him ten rubles change.

As Yuri headed for the exit, Amritzar followed him with his eyes, feeling ill at ease. This wasn't quite what he'd expected.

He would go back to his room, get his wife, and go for a stroll in the Arbat. For the time being, that was all he could do.

Like Aeroflot's fleet of Airbuses, its Sheremetyevo terminal was brand-new. Malko handed his passport to an immigration officer to be stamped. Thanks to his reservation at the Kempinski Hotel, he'd gotten a tourist visa in three days.

A few minutes later he had retrieved his suitcase and headed outside. He was immediately surrounded by a group of tough-looking men.

"You want taxi, sir?" one asked in English.

Malko turned to the man, who was wearing a long leather jacket.

"How much?"

"Six thousand rubles."

Malko smiled, and switched to Russian.

"You can cheat a foreigner, but not a Russian."

The man burst out laughing and said:

"All right, then. Twenty-five hundred."

The sky was dark, and it was spitting rain. As they drove along the endless Leningradsky Prospekt, Malko felt that Moscow hadn't changed much. There weren't any more old Lada 1500s or Volgas to be seen. The cars now were mostly Japanese, Korean, German, and occasionally French. But the buildings were still sooty-dark and plastered with gaudy advertisements.

And traffic was insane.

Once past Tverskaya Street, it really began to slow down. I should have brought Alexandra with me, thought Malko. This town is depressing.

Instead of *militsiya*, the blue-and-white police cruisers now bore the word "*Politsiya*" on their sides. The streets were lined with posters of the grim face of a right-wing politician, calling for votes for New Russia. They alternated with billboards showing a beautiful blonde in panties and push-up bra, advertising the bra for 499 rubles.

The city was also studded with huge artificial Christmas trees. The one in front of the Ministry of the Interior was taller than its statue of Lenin.

Malko's orders were simple: he was to stay away from the CIA offices at the embassy. Station Chief Tom Polgar, whom he knew well, would meet him that evening at the Kempinski with instructions.

Malko didn't quite see what his role was. This Amritzar business was strictly between the FBI and the FSB. If the agency wanted to play a dirty trick on the bureau, they could warn Amritzar that he was walking into a trap, but the FBI would never forgive them.

The taxi pulled up under the Kempinski awning. In a few moments Malko found himself in a fourth-floor suite with a view of the Kremlin towers and the golden domes of St. Basil's Cathedral at the end of Red Square.

It was a magical sight, with red stars gleaming on top of every steeple, and long red-brick walls surrounding the heart of Russian power. Malko remembered the huge Hotel Rossiya that long stood to the right of Red Square.

Malko went downstairs a half hour later, to find Polgar sitting in an armchair in the lobby.

"Hello, Malko. Did you have a good trip? Come on, I'll buy you dinner at the G."

A good choice: it was just a hundred yards away, and not crowded. In the dim light, the two men sat at the bar and ordered *zakuski* and vodka.

"Tom, I have to say that I'm not quite sure what I'm supposed to be doing here."

"Frankly, neither am I," said Polgar. "I asked you to come to be on the safe side. Maybe for nothing."

"Do you want to break up the deal between Amritzar and the FBI?"

"Nah, I can't do that. Even if the guy's innocent, he's got a bad attitude."

"So what are you hoping for?"

"I have a feeling the FSB is going to pull a fast one, but I don't know what."

"So what do I do?"

"For the moment, nothing. Maybe check out the Belgrade tomorrow. Scout the terrain."

"Do you know when the package is supposed to be delivered?"

"No, but it shouldn't be long. Because we're not officially involved, I can't ask the FBI or the FSB."

"That's not very encouraging," said Malko. "I can't hang around the Belgrade too long. I'll be noticed."

"I may have screwed up by asking you to come," said the station chief with a sigh. "Anyway you'll have an enjoyable trip."

"I was just as happy at home in Austria."

Polgar took a BlackBerry from his pocket and slid it over to Malko.

"Take this—you can use it to communicate with me. It's encrypted, like mine." The station chief stood up. "All right, I'll call you tomorrow."

"I still have a few friends here," remarked Malko. "I could look them up. Gocha Sukhumi, for example. He knows lots of people. If he's still alive, that is."

"Go ahead," said Polgar.

The first number Malko had for Sukhumi didn't answer, nor did the second. Gocha must've changed his cell phone, he thought.

He decided to try the landline, the one at Sukhumi's Moscow apartment.

A soft female voice answered, speaking Russian with a heavy Caucasian accent. Malko figured she was the busty Georgian woman who was Sukhumi's maid and occasional bedmate.

"Nadia?" asked Malko.

There was a brief silence on the phone and then the soft voice asked:

"Do you know me?"

"I'm a friend of Gocha's. You and I met two years ago. Is he there?"

"Yes, he's with a woman friend."

"I want to talk to him."

"Very well. Just a moment."

Nadia put the phone down, and Sukhumi's booming voice rang out a moment later.

"Malko! Where are you? Why don't you ever call me?"

"I'm here in Moscow, at the Kempinski."

"*Bozhe moy!* Come on over! I owe you big-time."

It was true. Years ago, Malko had given Sukhumi the names of the two men who killed the woman he was going to marry. In revenge, he gunned them both down. Apparently he was still feeling grateful.

"I'm on my way," said Malko. "Are you still at the same address?"

"Yes, I am."

The Georgian lived at the famed Dom na Naberezhnoy, the House on the Embankment. This was an imposing twelve-story gray building on the Bersenevskaya Embankment on the south bank of the Moskva River opposite the Kremlin. It had some five hundred apartments, stores, and a theater.

In Soviet times, the Dom was reserved for high-level apparatchiks, and their memory lived on in the bronze plaques with their profile on the front of the building. In a way, these were now memorial plaques, because many of the Dom tenants had come to a bad end, caught in the mad purges of the Stalin years.

When a black NKVD Volga stopped at the building—

always at night—it was to arrest another victim, who would wind up shot in the Lubyanka basement. In those days, you sometimes heard screams in the hallways while the other tenants, now thoroughly awake, held their breath, praying that the secret services men wouldn't stop at their door.

Times had changed.

The apartments had been privatized and were now occupied by foreigners or rich Russian businessmen like Sukhumi.

Malko slipped on his vicuña coat and went out. To get to Sukhumi's, he just had to walk along Sofiskaya Embankment, passing under the Bolshoy Kamenny Bridge.

"Malko!"

Sukhumi himself opened the door, and swept Malko up in a lung-crushing bear hug. Then he led him into the living room, whose windows looked out on the Kremlin on the other side of the Moskva.

The apartment hadn't changed. Bare white walls and little furniture, stacks of crates and cartons everywhere.

Sukhumi opened a bottle of Tsarskaya vodka and filled two shot glasses.

"*Na zdorovie!*" he cried.

They clinked glasses. Though velvety smooth, the Tsarskaya packed a punch.

Malko looked at Sukhumi. They had known each

other for a long time and had betrayed each other at various times. Malko had slept with Sukhumi's girlfriend Nina and was accidentally responsible for her death, which the Georgian had avenged.

"I was never able to tell you about that fucker Kaminski," Sukhumi was saying. "I put two bullets in his head."

"I suspected as much."

"Same with the other guy. At least those two knew why they were being killed. If you hadn't tipped me off, I would have never known. So I owe you. Do you need something?"

"I might," said Malko.

If anyone could find out about the FSB's plans, it would be Sukhumi.

In the days of the Soviet Union, he belonged to the Georgian KGB, and helped Georgian president Eduard Shevardnadze put down the rebellion in Abkhazia in 1993.

Later, a conflict with the regime arose, and Sukhumi resigned from the KGB to go into business. Thanks to his intelligence contacts, he'd managed to snag some of the very few oil export licenses available. Every week a train of tanker cars left the St. Petersburg area, bound for Finland.

The deal was very simple: Sukhumi bought the oil with rubles, but sold it for dollars.

In six months he'd amassed a small fortune by buying gas stations in Moscow, while staying close to the *siloviki*.

When Malko knew him in 1999, Sukhumi was in and out of the Kremlin, talking with Boris Yeltsin and Vladimir Putin and their advisors. At the time, he'd given Malko judicious advice that helped them stay alive.

The time had come to revive the relationship.

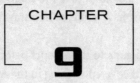

CHAPTER

9

Parviz Amritzar stood and went to admire the illuminated façade of the Ministry of Foreign Affairs. You didn't see buildings like that even in New York, he thought.

Then he sat back down at the tiny desk where he had spread his downloaded instructions on firing an Igla-S. This was hardly the first time he had read them, but now it was with new eyes. And he'd just noticed something he realized might be a problem. When he was acquiring the target, his hand couldn't afford to shake. If his aim was off by more than two degrees, the missile would miss its target.

It was the Igla's only weakness, and he intended to overcome it.

From now on, he would be counting the hours until Yuri called to say that he could take possession of the missile. The U.S. president would be coming to Russia in ten days. That was plenty of time for Amritzar to scout the attack locale and rehearse. It would be easy enough to find where and when Air Force One was landing.

Amritzar decided to go to bed. As he lay down, he

reached under the mattress to touch the envelope with the bundle of $200,000 that Mahmud had given him. The room didn't have a safe, so he always kept the money near at hand.

Benazir had gone to sleep hours before, exhausted by the miles they'd covered walking in the Arbat pedestrian arcade and along Novy Arbat, a wide avenue lined with stores and restaurants.

I should write her a letter explaining why I'm doing this before I go on my mission, Amritzar thought. She had her return plane ticket, and he would leave her his credit cards to pay the hotel bill.

He would never get to see his child, of course. . . .

But the idea of seeing the president's plane explode would be payment in full, finally avenging the members of his family killed by the American drone.

Gocha Sukhumi had already downed a third of the bottle of Tsarskaya along with some herring. His pleasure in seeing Malko again seemed sincere, as was his gratitude to him for fingering the men responsible for his fiancée's death. Shooting the two men had apparently brought him peace of mind.

He put his empty glass down on the table and glanced at the enormous gold watch dangling from his wrist.

"We're about to have a visitor," he announced.

"Your girlfriend?"

"Yeah. Julia Naryshkin. You'll see, she's a knockout. An intellectual, too. She lives in Peredelkino, that fancy writers' colony a couple of miles beyond the MKAD"—the Moscow Automobile Ring Road.

Malko was a little surprised to hear Gocha describe the woman as an intellectual. Sukhumi's taste usually ran more to the sexy minx, the down and dirty types.

The Georgian started when the doorbell rang.

"Hurray! She's here."

Thirty seconds later, a tall, beautiful redhead walked into the living room. She had long, curly hair and sea-green eyes. She was wearing the usual straight skirt over very high-heeled boots, but also a white blouse without a bra, which was unusual in Russia. Malko could make out her nipples under the fabric.

"*Ducheska!*" Sukhumi roared. "Meet Malko Linge, an old pal who's done a lot of stuff with me."

Julia's green eyes looked at Malko appraisingly.

"*Vui gavarite po russky?*"—Do you speak Russian?

"*Da.*"

This loosened up the atmosphere. Sukhumi had called his girlfriend "a little dove," but she was more like a hawk. She had a cold, forceful gaze and radiated strength. She might be an intellectual, thought Malko, but she's clearly a woman who knows what she wants.

And extraordinarily sexy, in spite of her fairly modest clothes.

"We're off to the Bolshoi," cried Sukhumi. "Let's go!"

"We're going to the opera?" asked Malko in surprise.

"No," said Julia. "It's a restaurant across the way."

Gérard de Villiers

Seated in one of the deep armchairs in the Metropol bar, Alexei Somov was already on his third vodka. Two tables away, a busty blonde in a split skirt was shooting him increasingly meaningful glances. If I snap my fingers, I bet she'll crawl over and give me a blow job, he thought. He impatiently looked at his watch. Razgonov was late, though the general was the one who had called the meeting.

Somov heaved a sigh, and met the blond woman's eye directly. She stood up and came to his table.

"Good evening," she said.

She was standing right in front of him, her splendid breasts out-thrust, a come-hither look in her eyes. Somov decided he felt like fucking her. Rummaging in his pocket, he fished out a magnetic room key and a wad of five-thousand-ruble bills, and stuffed them in her hand.

"Go up and wait for me in Room 212," he ordered. "I've got some business now."

The woman hesitated, and Somov felt he should make himself clear. He grabbed her thigh and roughly jammed his hand between her legs.

"Get going, now!"

The blonde sashayed her way to the elevators.

A minute later, the huge figure of the GRU general appeared. Razgonov dropped into a nearby armchair.

"Sorry I'm late," he said. "I had to go to the Kremlin."

"No sweat," said Somov. "Have you thought about our deal?"

Razgonov nodded.

"Yes, I have. The Kremlin has agreed to release an Igla-S from the Kolomna factory. They have about twenty in stock."

Somov looked surprised.

"I don't need just one missile," he said. "I need eight of them. I promised."

"*What*? That's much too risky!" exclaimed the general. "And I haven't completely made up my mind. I'm the one taking all the chances in this business."

"For eight million dollars," Somov pointed out. "In crisp new bills from Dagestan. With unrecorded serial numbers."

"When will I get the money?"

"As soon as I get back from there. You trust me, don't you?"

"Yes, of course," said the general wearily.

"So?"

Razgonov took the time to drink a shot of vodka before answering.

"I've taken care of one possible problem," he said. "The guy who handles the Igla-S inventory at the Kolomna plant is an old subordinate of mine, Anatoly Molov. He does what I tell him. If I ask him to take eight missiles out of inventory while listing only one, he'll do it. I just have to say the words 'special operation.' He's the only person who tracks the inventory, so it's no problem."

"That's great," said Somov. "When will this happen?"

"When I give him the official go-ahead to ship a missile to Moscow. That's all I can do for now."

"That's enough," said Somov. "I'll take care of the rest."

"Meaning what?"

"I'll pick up the missiles and truck them to Dagestan. Then wrap up the rest of the business there."

"And you guarantee they won't be used against our people?"

"You can count on me," said Somov with a reassuring smile.

Razgonov looked at him coldly.

"You realize that if these Iglas fall into the wrong hands, I'll become your worst enemy, right?"

"I know that." Somov paused. "Now that we're on the same page, I'll call you as soon as I'm ready. What about the Pakistani guy?"

"He's not our problem." The general finished his vodka and got to his feet. "I'll wait for word from you."

Somov stood up in turn and whispered:

"I've got a horny bitch waiting for me upstairs. You feel like having a little fun?"

"Some other time. I'm in a hurry."

The moment Razgonov left, Somov hurried to the elevator. When he knocked on the door of the room, it opened almost immediately.

The blonde had taken off her hat and gave him a look that suggested all the deadly sins—especially lust. Her breasts practically jumped into Somov's face, and he could feel himself getting hard. Without a word, he grabbed her breasts and flattened her against the wall.

She obediently reached for Somov's cock through his

pants, and tried to free it. Now grunting like a boar, he released her breasts and slipped a hand under her long skirt. A seam split, revealing her black stockings and the white skin of her thighs.

For her part, the woman had managed to pull the big cock out and was energetically stroking it.

With his left hand Somov tore off her panties. He bent his knees and almost without preamble shoved into her like a charging Cossack. She cried out.

While pounding away, he forced her down onto the bed. He flailed around for a moment, then came deep inside her.

The décor in the Bolshoi was modern, with pop music instead of classical. Julia, Sukhumi, and Malko were lounging on seats so deep that their mouths were practically level with the table. They were in the back room. It was cozier than the brightly lit front room, which faced the street.

"Anyone want some more Beluga?" asked Sukhumi.

Sprawled on a couch, he had a hand on his companion's thigh and was surreptitiously moving it upward. Seeming not to notice, Julia occasionally gave Malko the eye.

Sated, everyone refused the Beluga.

"Be honest, Julia," said Sukhumi. "Isn't this better than Dagestan?"

Turning to Malko, he said:

"Julia's old lover was the mayor of Makhachkala."

"Magomed wasn't my lover, he was my fiancé," Julia calmly corrected him. "He was a very nice man, and he loved me very much. Though it's true he was a bit brutal."

"Did he beat you?" asked Malko, amused.

"No, but he once killed one of his friends for saying something mean about his cat."

Clearly a touchy subject, thought Malko.

"What happened to him?"

"He had an accident in his car," said Julia. "He was crossing some railroad tracks when it blew up."

She explained that someone had buried a 550-pound FAB-250 fragmentation bomb under the tracks that went off when Magomed's armored Mercedes 600 drove over it.

"Was he killed?" asked Malko.

"No, he wasn't. The Mercedes split open like a mango, in spite of the armor plating. He was badly hurt, but he survived. Magomed's been in a wheelchair ever since, and he fled to Turkey so as not to be killed."

"Why were they after him?"

"He wanted to be president of Dagestan."

Sukhumi chuckled and explained.

"The Kremlin gives Dagestan two billion dollars every year to keep it in the Russian Federation, and the president spreads the money around. So of course everybody wants to be president."

A golden opportunity.

"He wanted me to convert to Islam," Julia continued. "That's why I left him."

Sukhumi chuckled again, more loudly.

"It was because he couldn't fuck you in his wheelchair anymore."

Gocha really doesn't have a lot of refinement, thought Malko. You don't make fun of the handicapped.

"All right," said Julia. "Let's go now."

She again gave Malko a long look. Either she was a born slut or she was trying to pick him up, for some unknown reason.

Sukhumi was counting out ten-thousand-ruble bills.

He and Julia went to the back of the Mercedes, and Malko was about to get in front with the driver when Sukhumi said:

"Come in back with us."

Julia shifted a little so the two men could fit on either side, and the car took off. Sukhumi drowsed, a hand on Julia's thigh. She turned to Malko and quietly said:

"You should come visit me in Peredelkino. I'm there most of the time, working."

Minutes later they were driving along the Moskva River.

"Gocha, I think I'm going to go home," said Julia, yawning. "I have to get up early tomorrow for an interview."

Sukhumi shook himself, like an enraged elephant.

"What the hell?"

"I've had a very nice evening," she assured him.

She kissed both Sukhumi and Malko and headed for a Mini parked nearby. Sukhumi tried to catch her, then came back to the Mercedes, irritated.

"What a bitch!" he growled.

"She knows how to handle men," remarked Malko. "Or else she's really tired."

"If you knew how hot she can be, when she's in the mood," said Sukhumi with a sigh. "It's like fire."

"I'm heading home too," said Malko. "But first I want to ask you something. Do you still have friends in the FSB?"

"A few."

"I'd like you to find out about something."

Malko told him about the Iglas. Sukhumi listened in silence.

"If it were anyone else asking, I'd tell them to fuck off," he said. "But you're a pal. I'll ask around."

CHAPTER

10

Bruce Hathaway had been cooling his heels in Colonel Tretyakov's office for fifteen minutes when the Russian officer came in.

"I'm sorry to keep you waiting," Tretyakov said, setting a heavy briefcase down. "I was held up."

The colonel was in civilian clothes and looked drawn and preoccupied. The FBI official assured him that waiting was no problem but that he was anxious to hear more. The fact that the head of the FSB's Fifth Directorate had asked him to come over meant that things were moving.

Tretyakov sat at his desk and opened a file his secretary had prepared for him.

"I have the approval for our operation," he announced. "We will be given a functioning Igla-S missile in three days, and you can 'sell' it to your Gospodin Amritzar."

"Wonderful," said the American. "How do we proceed?"

"We're not going to bring the missile to the Hotel Belgrade. That would be too complicated. Instead, it will be delivered to a garage on Batiski Street we sometimes use.

Gérard de Villiers

It's wired for sound and video recording, which should be useful for your operation."

In other words, a carefully prepared setting for the sorts of traps that the Russians so liked to set.

"Here is how I expect things will unfold," the colonel continued. "The Igla-S will be coming from the factory, which is about seventy miles from Moscow. It's a two-hour drive, so it should be here at eleven o'clock at the latest.

"I suggest that your agent 'Yuri' be in place before Amritzar arrives. Yuri will be accompanied by two agents from the Moscow FSB with the authority to arrest an arms dealer within Russia. He can introduce them to Amritzar as his partners."

"That seems perfect," said Hathaway. "Will the missile already be there?"

"It should arrive at the same time, but that doesn't matter. The people bringing it are just regular truck drivers, and they won't know what's going on.

"As requested, we will film the exchange of missile for money. Amritzar will hand Yuri two hundred thousand dollars in hundred-dollar bills in exchange for the Igla-S. At that point, our men will arrest him. He'll be taken to Lubyanka for interrogation, then imprisoned in Lefortovo. All you have to do then is to request his extradition to bring him to the United States for trial.

"I've discussed this with our attorney general, who will make sure everything goes smoothly. Will that be satisfactory?"

"I can't thank you enough," said Hathaway.

"I'm just following the 2003 protocol," said Tretyakov.

He closed his file and stood up, signifying that the meeting was over.

When Hathaway was in the elevator, he punched the cabin wall in a burst of joy. The FBI was going to score another spectacular success in the war on terror.

Tom Polgar met Malko at the Kalina restaurant, on the twenty-first floor of a modern high-rise on Novinsky Boulevard.

"Have you turned up anything new?" asked the station chief as soon as they had ordered their shashliks.

"Not yet, but I've put Gocha Sukhumi on the hunt."

"Do you trust him?"

"Not entirely, but he owes me a debt of honor, and I don't know anyone else who has such high-level contacts in the FSB. Of course, he may not turn up anything."

Polgar stared at his plate.

"I don't have any word from the FBI, either. They're keeping mum. Besides, they don't like us. Maybe I'm making a mistake. Can you think of another tack to take?"

"Beyond keeping an eye on Amritzar, no. And I'm not sure even that will give us much."

"I hope I didn't make you come to Moscow for nothing."

A waiter brought the shashliks.

Malko thought of Julia Naryshkin. If he was able to see her again, at least his visit to Moscow would give him that pleasure. He felt bad at the idea of stealing yet another woman from Gocha, but his hunter's instinct was too strong.

Carpe diem.

Amritzar crossed the intersection and started down the Arbat. Despite the chill wind sweeping the street, some stoic souvenir sellers had set up their stands. There were few tourists around. The Pakistani's hands were stuck in the pockets of his fur-lined jacket and his teeth were chattering. Yuri had phoned an hour earlier and told him to take a walk on the Arbat.

No specific rendezvous. He would be approached, he was told.

Amritzar had left his hotel, crossed the Garden Ring road, and entered the pedestrian street. He had now walked its length twice. He'd brought the $200,000 with him, just in case.

He was standing in the middle of the Arbat when he spotted Yuri coming in from a side street. He was wearing a sheepskin coat and had a *shapka* on his head. He fell into step beside him.

"You have news?" asked Amritzar.

"Yes. We can give you an Igla-S in three days," he said.

After an initial rush of excitement, Amritzar was seized by a sudden panic. What would he do with a surface-to-air missile at the Belgrade? The thing was nearly six feet long.

As if reading his mind, Yuri immediately said:

"I've arranged some things for you. Our organization will let you store the Igla-S in one of our garages until the day you use it. It'll be guarded by two *boiviki* who are making jihad. They speak a little English and they know how the missile operates. They can help you prepare your action."

"What about after that?"

"That depends on you," said Yuri with a slight smile. "If everything goes as planned, you can go back to your hotel and return to the United States. Otherwise, these men will look after you. They'll be returning to the Caucasus to continue their battle, and you can become a fighter. In Dagestan many foreigners are fighting by their side."

"Do you want the money right now?" asked Amritzar hesitantly.

Yuri frowned.

"No. You'll hand it over when you have the missile in your possession."

They stopped in the middle of the street near a stand that sold nesting *matryoshka* dolls. Yuri took a slip of paper from his pocket and gave it to him.

"Here's the address to go to. Make sure you aren't followed. Are you armed?"

"No."

"Come with me."

Yuri pulled Amritzar into a doorway, slipped something heavy into his hand, and said:

"All right. We'll meet at this address in three days."

Now alone, Amritzar looked down at what he'd been given: a big Makarov pistol. He immediately stuck it in his jacket pocket, then came out onto the street and headed for the Belgrade.

His life was changing; he could feel it. Gone were the days when he helplessly vented on the Internet. Now he was acting.

He wondered what he would tell Benazir.

Rem Tolkachev quickly read the short document that a man in gray had brought to his office. It was from Alexander Bortnikov. The FSB chief assured him that all measures had been taken so that Special Agent Jeff Soloway of the Moscow FBI, whom Parviz Amritzar knew as Yuri, would be arrested and charged with espionage. It was a tried-and-true Soviet tactic. Even if the charge was implausible, a good pretext would help with appearances. After that, things should go smoothly.

The Americans had a phobia about hostages, even in a country like Russia, Tolkachev knew. Every American citizen was sacred, especially one who had put his life on the line as a spy. And Russia was powerful enough to resist international pressure. The charge brought by the country's attorney general would give the arrest a veneer of legality that should quiet any critics.

Anyway, the Americans weren't crazy. Even if they immediately realized it was a setup, they knew they would have to kowtow to the FSB if they wanted to get Soloway back.

The exchange of spies in Vienna in July 2010 had created a precedent.

It was a workable formula: no money, no betrayal, and nobody admitted fault.

Feeling satisfied, Tolkachev lit one of his pastel cigarettes. He was pleased at the idea of getting Viktor Bout released. Bout might merely be an ex-GRU agent turned adventurer, but he was a Russian citizen.

Besides, some Americans hadn't realized that the Cold War had resumed, in more subtle shape. The Russians didn't miss communism, but the United States still represented absolute evil, as it had in the days of the Soviet Union.

Tolkachev took Bortnikov's report and went to store it in his safe.

It was dynamite.

Sukhumi's saucy maid with the big breasts opened the door for Malko.

"Gospodin Sukhumi isn't here yet," she said. "He phoned to say that he'll be late. There's another person waiting in the billiard room."

Malko knew the apartment's layout. When he reached the billiard room, he immediately spotted Julia Naryshkin's curly red hair.

Sukhumi had phoned three hours earlier to invite

him to dinner, saying he had something interesting to tell him. Malko hadn't expected either Gocha's lateness or Julia's presence.

"Good evening," she said, turning around.

She had changed her clothes and was now wearing a pair of jeans that looked sewed onto her. She still had no bra.

She looked at Malko confidently as he approached, took her hand, and kissed it.

Julia seemed pleased to see him.

"I didn't know you were coming," he said. "It's a very nice surprise."

"For me too," she said, gazing into his eyes.

She was flirting with him, yet she didn't have the profile of most oligarch girlfriends. There was no direct provocation, she clearly had a good brain, she was physically very attractive, and she had unmistakable inner strength.

What makes her tick? Malko wondered.

Theoretically, Gocha wasn't the kind of man Julia would be attracted to, yet she was his mistress. Was it for money? He'd heard she was financially independent. Her connection with the Dagestani strongman was strange, too.

While these thoughts were going through Malko's mind, Julia reached in her purse and took out a business card.

"I didn't have time to give you this last time," she said quite naturally.

Malko pocketed it just as the front door slammed. Thirty seconds later Sukhumi came into the billiard room. He ran over to her, put his arm around her waist, and pulled her close.

"*Dushenka!* How pretty you're looking!"

Slyly, he ran one of his big hands over her rump. The young woman gently pulled away and said:

"Your friend here has been waiting, too."

She hadn't changed expression. A woman with perfect self-control.

Sukhumi abruptly turned to Malko and said:

"Come on. We have to talk."

Taking Malko by the arm, Sukhumi led him into the room he used as an office. It was piled with cartons of vodka and littered with files. A Kalashnikov with a charger stood in a corner.

The Georgian kicked the door shut, dropped into a ratty old armchair, and lit a cigarette.

"I saw somebody last night," he said. "An old pal from before 'the man with the birthmark.'"

"So what did you hear?"

"You were right. Something's up."

"What?"

"I don't know the details, but the big shots in the FSB are licking their chops. Apparently it's a plan to screw the Americans, trap some FBI guy. They're thrilled. They've never had an American in Lefortovo before."

"What do they have in mind?

"I have no idea," Sukhumi admitted. "We've only heard rumors, but it seems serious. I can't ask any more questions, otherwise it'll come back and bite me."

Gérard de Villiers

"Thanks, Gocha. I appreciate this."

Malko now found himself facing a dilemma. Should he warn the FBI about what was going on? If he didn't, he became an accomplice to a Russian setup. If he did, the consequences could be even worse.

CHAPTER

11

Malko flashed Sukhumi a grateful smile.

"Thank you again, Gocha," he said. "And now I think I'll leave you with your girlfriend."

"What do you mean? Aren't you having dinner with us?"

"I can't. I have to pass on your information."

Tom Polgar absolutely had to be told.

Sukhumi wrested his bulk out of the armchair.

"What do you think of Julia?"

"She's charming."

The Georgian snorted.

"She's a lot more than that, to have survived in Dagestan! Magomed, the guy she was with, he's an animal, a killer. His pals, too. I think Julia enjoyed that."

"She had money," said Malko.

"Some, but she doesn't give a damn about that. Something else turns her on."

"What?"

"I don't know yet," said Sukhumi. "I'm still trying to find out. But I can tell you one thing: she's a volcano in the sack. When she's in the mood, that is. Come on, you can say good-bye to her."

Julia Naryshkin was still there, playing with the billiard balls.

"I'm afraid I have to leave," said Malko, kissing her hand and looking her in the eye. If he didn't already have her business card in his pocket, he would have been sorry to go.

The moment he was outside, Malko switched on his encrypted BlackBerry and called Polgar. The station chief answered immediately, talking over a background hubbub. He wasn't at the office.

"I need to talk to you," said Malko.

"Now?"

"Yes."

"I'm at the Café Ararat. A cocktail party where I have to see some people."

"I'm on my way."

"Want me to send my car?"

"I should be able to find a taxi. If I can't, I'll call you back."

Leaving the Kempinski, he walked a little way toward the bridge and raised his arm. A car driven by a woman pulled up, and Malko told her where he wanted to go.

"That'll be three hundred rubles," she said.

When he stepped out of the elevator, Malko encountered a dense crowd on the Café Ararat's terrace, which had a sweeping view of the Bolshoi theater and the city. As usual, there were plenty of gorgeous, haughty women, but they came with price tags. Looking around, Malko spied the CIA station chief deep in conversation with a fat man with glasses. Polgar quickly got free, and Malko led him over to a picture window.

"Did you find something out?" he asked.

Malko related Sukhumi's information, and Polgar gave a low whistle.

"Christ! I have to let Washington know."

"You could just step across the hall, Tom. The FBI is on the same floor as you at the embassy, isn't it?"

"I don't have the guts to do that," Polgar admitted. "Besides, what if they get suspicious? They're so paranoid. I can't tell them anything without approval from Langley."

"Suppose something disastrous happens in the meantime?"

Polgar shrugged.

"That's their problem. The bureau guys screw things up on their own time, and they don't tell us about it. If a life were at stake, I'd try harder, but that's not the case."

"Okay, but you've been warned," said Malko. "I really wonder what the FSB is cooking up."

"We'll find out soon enough," said Polgar soberly. "And by the way, I doubt Langley's going to let me talk to them."

"So what I did was pointless."

"Not at all! I'll go back to the office this evening and draft a report, and date-stamp it. That way, they'll know we figured out that the FSB was setting a trap.

"If we talk to the FBI now, it's sure to come back to

haunt us. Knowing the bureau, they might even accuse us of plotting with the FSB. And we would have to reveal our sources, namely you and Sukhumi. God knows where that would lead.

"Maybe this'll teach those jerks not to launch these crazy sting operations. They could just go out and find some real terrorists, instead of inventing them. We even have some spares, but they won't go after them.

"The FBI guys are bureaucrats, not real field agents. In the States, they flash their badges and think they can do anything. They act like they're above the law."

No doubt about it, Tom Polgar didn't like the FBI.

Malko heaved a sigh. He should have stayed at Gocha's with the alluring Julia Naryshkin.

For once, Rem Tolkachev stayed at his office late. The day before, shaking with fever from a cold, he'd only been able to put in a couple hours' work before heading home.

He was eager for a bowl of borscht at the Kremlin's Buffet Number 1, but first he had to go through the most recent documents delivered by the men in gray.

A brief report from the Border Guards brought Tolkachev up short. It told of the arrival in Moscow of one Malko Linge, a CIA operative who had often visited Moscow in the past. According to the form, he was staying at the Kempinski Hotel.

Tolkachev looked at the document thoughtfully. The name Malko Linge was all too familiar to him. The man had made several forays into Russia and wreaked a great deal of havoc. The secret services considered him an extremely dangerous, very professional adversary. The KGB and then the FSB had both recommended eliminating him, and had even tried, but without success. The thaw in relations between Russia and the United States had worked in Linge's favor.

In any case, major intelligence services very rarely killed each other's agents, which could launch tit-for-tat reprisals. Mistakes were sometimes made in the heat of action, of course, but that wasn't the same thing.

Pensively, Tolkachev put down the Border Guards' report. Linge's presence in Moscow couldn't be happenstance, and he was too experienced an agent to come here without a good reason.

There was just one explanation: the CIA had gotten wind of the operation he was planning against the FBI. But how?

The FSB's request for information about Amritzar must have piqued the agency's curiosity, and it sent its point man to investigate. The crucial question was: Could Linge derail the operation Tolkachev had designed?

He carefully went over the operation in his mind. The trap was already set, and everything would be over two days from now. No matter how brilliant Linge might be, it would be impossible for him to interfere on the Russian side. Somehow he would have to get the information from his Moscow sources, and then warn the FBI.

Just in case, Tolkachev wrote a brief note to the FSB's Second Directorate, which tracked foreigners, ordering it to immediately start close surveillance of Linge.

But then the old spymaster wondered if he wasn't passing up an unexpected opportunity. After all, Linge was an enemy of Russia. Eliminating him could only be for the good. The trick was to dress it up so that it wouldn't look like a murder.

He rang for a man in gray and gave him the note. Then he switched off his office lights and headed for the buffet.

This was no time for him to be sick.

Malko gazed at the Kremlin towers, fascinated as always by this symbol of power that had endured through the centuries. Traffic moved slowly below the high red-brick walls. They didn't even look defended, and in fact the Kremlin grounds were open to the public.

The ring of his cell made him jump.

"I'm downstairs," said Polgar.

The station chief had ordered coffee and was looking at the almost empty lobby.

"I thought I would hear from you sooner," said Malko. It was almost six p.m.

"Time difference," said Polgar shortly. "It took Langley a while to think things over, and almost certainly consult with the White House."

"So?"

"We don't move. The agency feels that your information isn't specific enough for us to alert the FBI. The bureau might think it was a setup on our part, which would kick off an endless round of administrative infighting."

Malko found the whole thing infuriating, but he held his tongue.

"I'm positive Gocha is right," he finally said.

"Maybe, but we can't reveal him as a source. It would put his life in danger." Polgar shook his head. "We're closing this one down, Malko. You may as well go back to your castle."

"But what if something really bad happens? Say an FBI agent is arrested or killed?"

"Too bad," said Polgar indifferently. "They screw up, they pay for it."

The station chief's decision sounded final.

"In that case I'll leave as soon as I can get a flight. After stopping at Eliseevskiy to stock up on herring and red caviar, of course."

"Take your time," said Polgar amiably. "The information you got is useful. We have it on record, so if something goes wrong, we can use it to underscore the FBI's stupidity."

With friends like that . . . The two men fell into a rueful hush.

This situation is insane, thought Malko to himself. The CIA is getting into bed with the FSB over a turf war!

"I have to go," said Polgar. "Let me know when you're leaving town, and we'll have lunch together. Officially."

Malko was about to hang up when a woman's voice said "*Da?*"

"Is this Julia?"

"Who's calling, please?"

"Malko Linge."

"How nice of you to call," she said with a light, rippling laugh. "I was about to go out."

"Are you free for dinner?"

"I'm afraid not. I'm heading for Radio Moscow. I have a one-hour broadcast, so I'll be finishing very late."

"I don't mind," said Malko. "I'd really like to see you again."

"So would I, but another time. How about tomorrow?"

"Sure. What should we do?"

"I live pretty far away. Why don't I meet you at the Kempinski around seven?"

"Perfect."

After a pause, she added:

"Best not to mention this to Gocha. He's very jealous."

She hung up before Malko could comment.

He didn't feel like spending the evening alone. Suddenly he thought of Alina Portansky, the paralyzed painter's wife who had helped him so much during his last assignment. She had risked her life—and her virtue—to assist him.

He found her number in his phone's memory and dialed it, but a recorded voice announced that the number was no longer in service. This caused him a twinge of anxiety. Alina had stood up to the security services' pressure and had refused to accept any protection.

What had happened to her?

He couldn't leave Moscow without finding out.

He knew generally how to get to the Portanskys' place, but he couldn't recall the name of their street.

The Kempinski bellman called him a taxi.

"I'm going to Petrovsky Boulevard," Malko said to the driver. "I'll tell you where."

A few moments later he said:

"Stop here."

Malko had just recognized the little street where the Portanskys lived. He handed the driver four hundred rubles and started walking.

Another taxi stopped right behind him, and a husky man with a black watch cap pulled down to his ears got out. He looked right and left, as if getting his bearings.

Malko turned onto the street, and walked around a Dumpster. A hundred yards on, he looked back and saw the man with the black cap again. He was now walking behind him, his hands in his pockets.

Malko's pulse picked up.

There were no coincidences in Moscow, and Malko knew the secret services well enough to beware of them. When he reached the intersection of the street where Alina lived, he turned and sprinted down it as fast as he could.

He wasn't armed, and the man behind him certainly didn't wish him well. Halfway down the street, Malko looked back to see the man round the corner and start running after him. Now the situation was unmistakable.

Reaching the building door, Malko frantically punched in the apartment code, but it didn't work. The heavy metal door was ajar, so he ran inside to the elevator and closed the cabin's grill doors. The ancient mechanism lurched into movement as the front door flew open. The man in the watch cap ran toward the rising elevator, a long dagger in his right hand. He had hooded eyes in a pale, brutal face.

He grabbed the elevator doors and tried to pry them open. Failing that, he stuck his knife through the grill, slashing around at random.

The elevator rose with exasperating slowness. Meanwhile, the man turned and ran for the staircase. Malko's stomach was in knots. If Alina had moved, he was doomed. Looking down, he could see the man sprinting up the stairs. When the elevator reached the fifth floor, the killer was on the third. Malko burst out of the elevator and ran to the Portanskys' apartment door. Ignoring the keypad, he rang the bell.

Once. Twice. Three times.

The man was now just one floor below him.

Malko glued his ear to the door, but heard nothing, then stepped back to see how close his attacker was.

A creak made him turn around. The door was opening.

CHAPTER

12

"Who's there?" came a woman's voice, low but firm.

Wheeling around, Malko could see a woman in the shadows.

"Alina, is that you?" He was gasping for breath.

The door now opened completely, and the room light fell on him. Now on the threshold, Alina cried:

"Malko!"

Then she had her arms around him. As usual, she had her hair in a bun and was wearing a long dress, buttoned down to her ankles. She pressed against him, muttering something, kissing his neck like a cat.

Behind Malko, the heavy steps of his pursuer were getting closer. Grabbing her by the arm, he pushed her inside, then slammed the door and locked it.

"What's going on?" she asked.

"Somebody's after me."

Just then, the man outside started pounding on the door.

Alina yelled, "I'm calling the police!"

That must have given the attacker pause, because silence fell.

"I never thought I'd see you again," Alina said. She had stars in her eyes.

"Neither did I," admitted Malko. "Your phone was disconnected. I thought something must have happened to you."

"It was no big deal," she said with a smile. "The Moscow FSB questioned me a few times. Reminded me that it was a crime to consort with enemies of Russia. After that, they left me alone. Then I changed my phone number."

"Where's Alexei?"

"He's in the hospital again," she said sadly. "He's not doing very well. He stopped painting."

Alexei Portansky had been ill for some time. From the pain in Alina's face, Malko could tell she was worried about him.

She hugged him again, this time pressing her hips against his.

"I'm so happy to see you!" Then she added, biting her lip, "You're still doing dangerous stuff."

It wasn't meant as a criticism, and Malko smiled.

"It's my life."

Suddenly she pulled him even tighter. Her mouth moved over his face, found his lips and tongue. She started kissing him passionately.

He remembered how exciting Alina had been, with her small, firm breasts and welcoming hips. When he brushed against her stiff nipples, she let out a little cry, then reached down and grabbed his crotch.

"Come with me," she whispered. "It's been so long since I've made love."

Taking his hand, she led him into a dimly lit bedroom. She threw herself on the bed and pulled up her dress. Then she slipped off her white panties and dropped them on the floor.

When Malko entered her, she gave a whispery sigh, tightening her arms around him and raising her hips. Her legs were spread and she was trembling.

"*Bozhe moy*, that's so good! Come on!"

She was wet, and open to him.

Malko's excitement gradually rose to match Alina's joyful eagerness. He bent her thighs back and started thrusting into her vertically. A few moments later, he came.

They lay silently for a few moments.

Eventually, Alina's voice brought Malko back to earth.

"I'm hungry, but I only have some herring," she was saying. "Would you like some?"

"I love herring," he said, easing himself out of her.

"Stay there, and I'll fix us something. I have a little vodka too."

Lying in bed with his eyes wide open, Parviz Amritzar couldn't get to sleep. These might be the last peaceful hours of his life, he realized. Tomorrow at eleven he and

Yuri would pick up the Igla-S, and his whole life would change.

Amritzar turned his head and looked over at Benazir, who was sleeping on her side. He hadn't told her anything yet. If everything went well today, he would pay for the missile and come back to her in the hotel. The actual attack wasn't until the end of the following week, when Air Force One was due. Between now and then, he would have time to explain the path he had chosen.

He got out of bed and once again admired the illuminated mass of the Ministry of Foreign Affairs building across Smolenskaya Street. Moscow was growing on him, he realized.

But he was still too tense to sleep. What if Yuri stood him up?

He stepped into the bathroom and went back to reading the Igla-S technical manual. Suddenly the letters blurred before his eyes, and he realized he was crying.

Without quite knowing why.

It briefly occurred to him that instead of going to the meeting with Yuri, he could leave Russia on the first flight back to the United States. Then, to avoid al-Qaeda's anger, he would return the $200,000 to Mahmud.

But that would mean giving up his dream of revenge.

Malko looked out at the darkened street and shivered. It was almost midnight. After snacking on herring and pickled mushrooms, he and Alina had made love again. This time she had taken off her long dress with its dozens of buttons and enthusiastically yielded to all of Malko's fantasies, offering him her mouth, her ass, and again, her pussy.

She left him at the elevator, her lips against his, murmuring:

"*Ya tebya lyublyu*"—I love you.

Now Malko was back in the cold—and the danger. The street appeared deserted, however.

He walked to Petrovsky Boulevard and, by luck, was able to hail a taxi right away. Five hundred rubles got him back to the Kempinski.

There were no cops around, and nobody waiting for him, but he didn't feel safe until he was upstairs in his room. The brush with the man with the black watch cap meant he was under surveillance.

Good thing Tom gave me the encrypted BlackBerry, he thought as he dialed it.

It took the station chief a long time to answer.

"What's going on, Malko? It's past midnight!"

"I know. But somebody tried to kill me tonight."

He gave Polgar the details of the attack, then headed for the shower, trying to figure out why someone would want him out of the way.

It was only seven in the morning, but there were already a lot of cars in the KBM parking lot near the Oka River.

The river was the shining heart of Kolomna. It was a neat, prosperous little town, with a red-brick kremlin, wide avenues, shiny trams, and a modest statue of Lenin.

This was the real Russia.

Arzo Khadjiev was sitting behind the wheel of a yellow Lada 1500 parked opposite a Vera store with an odd pink façade. The young Dagestani with the fox-like face was watching the only entrance to the KBM factory, which sprawled across a lot on the banks of the Oka, some distance from downtown.

Vehicles would come out of the gate, drive uphill from the river along the big white factory building, and merge onto the city streets.

Two brass plaques at the gate informed visitors that the factory had been awarded the orders of Lenin and Red Star during the Great Patriotic War. Originally it had been a cement plant, built on Stalin's orders. Only later did it become a missile research and development center.

Operating under the unremarkable name Konstruktion Buro Manufaktura, KBM was the place where next-generation surface-to-air missiles were developed. These included the Igla-S used by the Russian military and widely sold abroad. They were manufactured in Izhevsk, in the Urals, but prototypes and small batches were produced at KBM.

Suddenly Khadjiev stiffened. A black Volga van had just emerged from the factory gate and was climbing the hill toward him. When it passed him, Khadjiev glimpsed two men inside. He grabbed his cell phone, spoke a few words, and took off after it.

The van drove along Maktova Avenue by a big McDonald's drive-through, a row of colorfully painted wooden *izbas*, and some typical fifteen-story apartment buildings.

Then it turned onto Leninsky Avenue, passing the town's handsome kremlin and a church with green and yellow domes. Glittering in the rising sun, they almost looked like gold.

Khadjiev again picked up his cell, this time to relay the license plate with the Kolomna prefix of the van he was following.

The two vehicles drove around a long green tram and took the road leading to the M5 Moscow–Chelyabinsk highway.

The van passed a gas station and took the on-ramp toward Chelyabinsk. But within a few miles it took an exit that circled around and under the highway, leading to an on-ramp in the Moscow direction. A light haze lay on the nearby forest. The area was completely deserted.

Khadjiev watched the black van slow to take the turn and go under the highway.

As it entered the sunken passageway, a Mercedes truck coming the other way suddenly appeared and blocked its path.

Dmitry Pankov, the van driver, cursed and slammed on the brakes. The big truck seemed to have skidded, and was now stopped across the roadway.

"*Bozhe moy!*" growled the driver. "What an asshole!"

He honked his horn, but the other driver didn't move. Pankov could see three men in the truck. Its passenger-side door opened, and a man got out and started walking toward him. He was wearing a fur-lined jacket, a watch cap, and jeans.

"I wonder what this jerk wants," snapped Pankov's passenger, the KBM shipping escort. Then he noticed that another vehicle, an old yellow Lada, had pulled up behind them, hemming them in.

"I don't like the looks of this," he said tensely. "Call the factory."

Just as Pankov reached for the radio, his door was yanked open. He only had time to see a swarthy man's unshaven face, then just the pistol with the silencer aimed at him. In his last moment of consciousness he heard a soft *pfut!*

The shipping escort raised an arm to protect himself, and it took the first bullet. The second one blew the top of his skull off.

Two more men jumped out of the Mercedes truck, raced around to the back of the KBM van, and threw its cargo doors open.

Standing next to the Lada, Khadjiev watched the off-ramp behind him.

This was the critical moment.

"*Davai, davai!*"—hurry up!—he yelled.

Stacked in the van were eight long, square cases. The men hauled them out and carried them to the Mercedes truck, running.

The entire operation took no more than two minutes. Slamming the truck's cargo doors shut, the three men jumped in. It backed out of the underground passageway, made a quick U-turn, and took the M5 on-ramp toward Moscow.

Khadjiev got into his Lada, drove around the stopped KBM van, and took the same on-ramp, racing to catch up with the Mercedes.

No one had witnessed the attack. The sunken passage under the highway couldn't be seen from the road or the nearby fields, which were empty in any case.

Within moments, the two vehicles were speeding toward Moscow together, and Khadjiev relaxed. If a pursuit were launched on the M5, it would be sent south, toward the Caucasus. It would never occur to the cops that someone might steal missiles and bring them to Moscow.

As he drove, Khadjiev took his cell phone, dialed a number, and had a very short conversation.

They were on a roll.

CHAPTER

13

Jeff Soloway exited the American embassy by the north gate and undertook the most perilous part of his mission: getting across the Garden Ring. He waited for a red light, then sprinted across the wide avenue to join the FSB agents in a blue Opel parked near a drugstore on the other side.

Even on their best days, Moscow drivers view pedestrians as a species of noxious vermin. Which is why most people on foot use the tunnels under the major avenues.

Panting, Soloway reached the Opel and got in. The FSB agent next to the driver turned around and said:

"Good morning, I'm Anatoly Chelovev from the FSB. We'll drive you to the rendezvous. Where is Gospodin Amritzar?"

"He's meeting us there. Is everything ready?"

"Yes."

"Do you have the device?"

"It's on its way."

The driver pulled out and merged with the crowded ring road traffic.

Soloway was nervous. Months of effort were coming to a head, and he wanted everything to go smoothly.

"What are your exact instructions?" he asked.

"We're taking you to the workshop where the missile will be delivered," the Russian said in a neutral tone. "You'll give the signal to go into action. As soon as you get the money from Amritzar and decide everything is in order, you'll identify yourself as an FBI agent. We'll then display our badges, identify ourselves as FSB, and arrest him.

"Amritzar will be taken to the Lubyanka for interrogation, and then jailed at Lefortovo. The attorney general will send you the file along with the audiovisual evidence. How does that sound?"

"Great!" said the excited American.

Soloway relaxed until the moment when the Opel slowed and passed through a gateway leading to Malya Street. As is common in Moscow, the entrance gave access to roads to apartment buildings scattered over several acres.

The car stopped in front of a workshop with a big wooden door with flaking paint and a sign that read "Garage." The two FSB agents got out. One opened the door and switched on the lights.

It certainly looked like a garage. It was about twenty by fifty feet, with crates and a big table in the center. An old Volga stood on blocks in a corner. The place smelled of dust and motor oil.

"This is one of the places we use," said one of the agents. "Everything can be taped and filmed."

"Where's the missile?" asked Soloway.

"Don't worry, it's on its way. It's coming from outside Moscow, and the traffic is bad. Want a cup of chai?"

"No, thanks."

The two Russians stepped into a glassed-in back office to make the tea.

Soloway lit a cigarette to calm his nerves, then called Bruce Hathaway.

"We're all set," he said, without giving any details.

"Call me as soon as it's done," said the FBI chief. Hathaway was also feeling tense. Because of the time difference, Washington was still asleep. He figured the operation would be wrapped up by the time FBI headquarters opened.

A black Audi sedan pulled up and parked about twenty yards from the garage door. Inside were four Moscow FSB agents, ready to arrest Soloway as soon as he received the $200,000 from Amritzar. Alerted by their colleagues in the FSB, they would charge him with espionage, for trying to obtain a missile covered by defense secrecy laws.

Since an FBI agent in Moscow didn't have diplomatic immunity, they could interrogate Soloway as long as they wanted to, and his protests wouldn't make any difference. The attorney general had been alerted and would pursue the matter as ordered.

What happened after that wasn't the FSB's concern.

The Audi left its motor running. The few passersby who noticed the car gave it a wide berth.

———

Rem Tolkachev had a report on the previous night's events in front of him. It didn't make for satisfactory reading. The Spetsnaz assigned to liquidate Malko Linge had totally failed in his mission. Though unarmed, the CIA man had managed to get away and return to the Kempinski.

Tolkachev could have Linge arrested there, of course, but on what pretext?

It would be stupid to attack him now, the spymaster decided. In two hours, the trap he'd set for the FBI would be sprung, and Linge's presence hadn't upset the plan. Tolkachev decided to write the operation off for now and settle the CIA agent's fate later.

His mind at ease, he turned his attention to other reports.

In the passageway under the M5 highway, three *politsiya* cruisers surrounded the black KBM van; one of its doors was still open.

A passing motorist, who'd been forced to drive around it, had called the police a half hour earlier. The van driver lay slumped against the steering wheel and appeared to have fainted.

A black Volga now joined the police cars, and two men stepped out, looking serious. One showed them his business card. He was Ivan Babichev, the KBM plant manager.

"What's going on?" he asked.

The *politsiya* sergeant pointed to the van.

"The two people in the vehicle were shot and killed at close range," he said. "Nobody saw or heard anything. Doesn't make sense, since the van was empty."

"Empty?" shouted Babichev, shaken.

Then he got a grip on himself.

"This van was carrying extremely sensitive equipment," he said. "It's been stolen."

He couldn't believe it.

Stepping aside, he called the Kolomna FSB chief. This was a matter of state security. Only terrorists could have stolen the missiles, he knew. The thought gave him goose bumps.

In moments, he had the officer on the line.

"I'll set up roadblocks on every highway heading south," the FSB chief immediately said.

South meant the Caucasus.

The rebels down there usually got this kind of gear by buying it from Russian troops stationed in Chechnya or Ingushetia. This was the first time any had been stolen near Moscow.

Through the taxicab window, Parviz Amritzar studied the front of the building. It was number 45, all right, and he recognized the wooden garage door Yuri had described.

Amritzar paid the five hundred rubles and got out. He

immediately started shivering, partly from the freezing Moscow weather, partly from nervousness.

His heart in his throat, he rapped on the wooden door. When it creaked open, his pulse shot higher. But seeing Yuri standing in the doorway, he relaxed. Entering the garage, he found it as cold inside as outside.

Amritzar was surprised to see two other men in the office.

"Who are those people?"

"Friends of mine," said Soloway. "My bodyguards."

"Is the Igla-S here?" Amritzar asked anxiously. "I have the money."

"It's coming with the men who will look after you. Do you want some tea?"

Amritzar shook his head no. He couldn't have swallowed a thing. The garage was plunged in icy cold and metallic silence. He had brought the Makarov pistol Yuri gave him but figured he had no need for it. In an hour he would be back at the Belgrade with Benazir. For her safety, he had decided to send her back to the United States after he explained why he was staying behind.

Leaning against an empty workbench, he said:

"Let me give you the money right away, Yuri. That way it'll be done."

"No, no, later," said Soloway. "I trust you. Mahmud said you were an honest jihadist."

The two men smoked cigarettes. They didn't have much to say to each other.

Suddenly a ringing cell phone startled Amritzar. It

belonged to one of the men in the office. After a long conversation, the man came out and pulled Yuri aside, ignoring Amritzar.

A few moments later Yuri came over to him. He looked serious and was obviously annoyed.

"There's been a problem," he said. "The people bringing the missile had to turn around. We have to put off the meeting."

"To when?"

"I don't know. I'll let you know. You can go back to your hotel."

Taking Amritzar by the arm, Soloway led him to the door.

"I'll phone you," he promised. "Walk over to Misaya Street. I'm sure you'll find a taxi there."

Feeling shaken, Amritzar started walking along the snow-lined road. He paid no attention to a black Audi with tinted windows that took off and drove away.

The Mercedes truck pulled into the courtyard of an old prewar building at 57 Lesnaya Street. To the right of the entrance stood a small shop with a sign that read "Caucasian Fruits—Wholesale." With its dusty windows, it looked abandoned. A small flight of metal stairs led from the courtyard down to the store's basement. The truck pulled around and parked next to it. The three men opened its back doors. Within minutes they had carried the eight cases from the KBM van down to the basement.

Two of them climbed back in the truck, which drove out of the courtyard. The third man stayed with the missiles.

Ten minutes later a Mercedes parked in front of the store. A tall man got out—it was Alexei Somov—and knocked on the store door. He was let in immediately.

He went down to the basement and examined the eight Igla-S cases. The first part of the job had been accomplished.

"You two, stay here," Somov ordered. "I'm going to arrange the rest of the trip."

Bruce Hathaway was baffled. He couldn't understand why his sting operation had failed.

"So they're going to phone you?" he asked, looking up at Soloway.

"They promised to," said the FBI agent. "It must be a technical problem. Nothing serious."

"And Amritzar didn't suspect anything?"

"I don't think so."

"Where is he?"

"I told him to go back to his hotel, that I'd let him know when the next meeting would be."

"Well, I'm going to talk to Tretyakov and find out what's up."

The moment Soloway left his office, Hathaway phoned the Fifth Directorate. The colonel's secretary said he wasn't available but would call back soon.

Eating breakfast in the Kempinski's restaurant, Malko kept an eye on the door, half expecting FSB agents to burst in at any moment.

He had a lunchtime meeting with Tom Polgar, which gave him a certain amount of cover. After that, he would have to decide. His mission in Russia was over, so he could catch an Aeroflot flight to Vienna later in the day. Or he could have dinner with the beautiful Julia Naryshkin.

If the FSB doesn't show up, I'll see Julia, he decided. The curly-haired redhead with the piercing eyes attracted and intrigued him. If she slept with him, it wouldn't be for a handful of rubles. Malko could detect in her a drive rarely found in men or women.

He was hooked on a woman he'd only seen twice, without the slightest physical contact.

The trickiest possible situation.

Tolkachev had been on the phone for nearly an hour, trying to find out what had happened. Gradually the facts started to emerge.

Someone had attacked the KBM truck carrying the Igla-S to Moscow as part of the trap he had set for the FBI. At this point, there was no way of knowing who was behind the theft, but it was a serious problem. The operation against the FBI was strictly need-to-know, so how could anyone have arranged the hijacking?

According to the Kolomna FSB, it was a professional job. Both murders had been committed with the same 9 mm pistol.

Why?

With the hijacking, Tolkachev's trap had collapsed like an overcooked soufflé. Everyone had gone home. The FBI to the American embassy, Amritzar to his hotel, and the FSB people to Bolshaya Lubyanka.

While awaiting fresh orders from on high, Tolkachev decided it was impossible to continue until he knew who had penetrated the operation.

Just in case, he asked Alexander Bortnikov and the GRU's commanding general, Anatoly Razgonov, to come in.

The one thing that escaped Tolkachev was the exact role played by Malko Linge.

Did he have anything to do with this fiasco?

CHAPTER

14

"What the fuck is going on, Alexei?" yelled Ana-
toly Razgonov. The general's voice was shaking, and his
face contorted with rage.

Alexei Somov managed to keep his cool. It was late
afternoon, and the two men were the only customers in
the Metropol bar. The bartender huddled behind the
counter, making himself as inconspicuous as possible.
When you're around the GRU, it's best to mind your own
business.

"What exactly are you talking about?" asked Somov
calmly.

"I'm talking about the two guys who got blown away
in Kolomna, you dipshit! They weren't *chernozopie* rag-
heads, either. They were good Russians. I warned you,
Alexei: no screw-ups!"

Just then, a folksinger in a long multicolored dress
took a stool at the bar, and the sad strains of her *bayan*
accordion began to fill the air. She was playing an old, sad
tune about birches and steppes without end.

Somov leaned across the table.

"Did you really want people to know that the van was carrying *eight* Iglas, and not just one? I'm sorry, Anatoly, but it was the only way. Now only one person knows how many missiles left the factory, the guy who wrote 'one' in his inventory logbook. You said you trusted him. Is that still true?"

"Yeah, it's true," said Razgonov.

"All right, then. You'll feel better when you get your money. You can't make an omelet without breaking eggs."

In Chechnya, Somov and his unit had broken a lot of eggs.

But Razgonov was still angry.

"I've been called in by Rem Tolkachev," he growled, shaking his head. "What the fuck am I supposed to tell him?"

"You could try the truth," said Somov sarcastically. "If you want to be sent downstairs in the Lubyanka, that is."

Razgonov didn't bother to reply. The *bayan* continued to spread its sadness.

Suddenly Somov had an idea.

"Hey, what about the pigeon, that Pakistani American guy? He was going to pay two hundred thousand dollars for the Igla-S. You think he still has the money?"

The question took Razgonov by surprise.

"I have no idea," he said. "Why?"

"Because if we could get our hands on it, the two hundred thousand dollars would make a nice pension for those two KBM guys' families."

"How are you going to manage that?"

"I have a plan, and it ought to work."

Without meaning to, Colonel Tretyakov's secretary Anna had given Somov two useful pieces of information: Parviz Amritzar's name and the hotel where he was staying. It was enough to set a trap for him.

"Just hang tight for a while," Somov told Razgonov. "This will all be nailed down in a week or two, and you'll have the money you need. And if everything works out, those two widows will have enough to live on."

When the two men parted, the mood was chilly. They were in it together now, for better or for worse.

Amritzar returned to the Hotel Belgrade as night fell, having taken Benazir to admire the store windows on Tverskaya Street. He was feeling rattled and found it hard to make conversation. The failure of the morning's meeting had left a sour taste in his mouth.

Just as they entered their room, the phone on the night table rang. Amritzar ran over to answer it.

"Parviz?" came a man's voice.

"Yes, who—?"

"I'm calling for Yuri. He straightened things out."

Amritzar felt a rush of happiness.

"Really?" he asked incredulously.

"Yes, and he's waiting for you right now."

"Where?"

"Take a taxi to the intersection of Gogoldin Boulevard

and Petrovka Street. We'll meet you there. Be sure to bring the money."

"I'm on my way!"

Amritzar hung up and turned to Benazir.

"I have an urgent appointment," he said. "I have to go out again."

She didn't argue, and he ran to the elevator.

By good luck he found a real, legal taxi on Smolenskaya. The driver even spoke a little English.

The old buildings flew by as if in a dream, until the taxi stopped at an unremarkable intersection. Amritzar got out and went to wait in front of a store selling fur coats and *shapkas*.

Five minutes later, a big man in a black leather coat appeared, bareheaded despite the cold. He had a square face with expressionless, almond-shaped eyes and stood a good ten inches taller than Amritzar.

"Parviz?"

"That's right."

"Yuri is expecting us," Alexei Somov said in quite good English. "Do you have the money?"

"Yes."

"Then come with me."

He led Amritzar to a double-parked Mercedes, and they got in. Silence reigned during their trip. Eventually the car entered the inner courtyard of a building and stopped.

Amritzar looked around nervously.

"This isn't where we were this morning," he said.

"That's right," said the tall man. "We had to change locations. Follow me."

He had Amritzar take the metal stairs down to the basement of a store. The dim light from a single hanging bulb revealed a tall man on a stool who stood as Amritzar came down the stairs. His narrow face and sharp chin made him look shifty.

"Arzo here will take care of you," said Somov. "Go with him to the stairs in the back."

Amritzar picked his way through the gloom toward the back of the basement, with Khadjiev on his heels. He didn't see him pull a 9 mm Makarov semiautomatic with a long silencer from his belt.

The single shot to Amritzar's neck hardly echoed on the heavy basement walls. He collapsed in a heap.

With Khadjiev's help, Somov rolled Amritzar onto his back and began to search him. He quickly found and pocketed the envelope full of dollars.

"Wrap him in plastic," he said. "It's so cold, it'll be okay. You can load him in with the equipment and dump him somewhere along the way."

The forests of the Caucasus were littered with graves, unknown and unclaimed.

After Somov left, Khadjiev searched the body again. He found some Russian money, a watch, and a ring. He took Amritzar's cell phone, too. He doesn't need it anymore, he thought, and every little bit helps.

Though stuck in traffic, Somov was in high spirits. He had a date with Anna, who had turned him on to this profitable business. She would provide some excellent sexual recreation. In addition, he had kept his promise to Razgonov, and now had enough money to pay for the operation's collateral damage. He wasn't going to take a penny of the $200,000 destined for the widows. Knowing the Russian soul, he doubted they would long mourn their dead.

Tom Polgar's gray Chevrolet was idling on the Sofiskaya Embankment below the bridge, and Malko jumped in. They had arranged the meeting only minutes before, to avoid being followed. Now, caught in the traffic on the Kamenny Bridge, the car was crawling along.

"Why do you think they tried to kill you?" asked Polgar.

"I have no idea. I haven't done anything aside from get the information I gave you, and which you didn't use. Unless somebody wanted to take advantage of my being in Moscow to take me out, because of my past activities. I'm not working on any active cases, so it would be easy to make it look like an ordinary crime."

"Well, I think it's pretty suspicious," said the station chief. "The sooner you catch a plane out of here the better."

"That's what I'm planning," said Malko. "I have a flight tomorrow evening."

"I'll send a car to take you to the airport," said Polgar. "It'll be safer. An attempt like this could only come from on high, from the Kremlin. They might have other nasty plans for you."

"I'll be careful," promised Malko. "How about you? What's going on with the FBI?"

"Not a thing. All quiet on the bureau front. It's as if their operation was canceled. If it had worked, it would be in the papers, and their boys would be walking around thumping their chests.

"I'll drive you back to the Kempinski now. By the way, this'll probably be the last time we'll see each other in Moscow. I'm going back to Langley in six months, to run the Eastern Europe desk."

They passed the Borovitsky gate, drove up along the Manege and around Red Square, then headed back toward the south bank of the Moskva.

Stunned, Bruce Hathaway reread the email he'd just gotten from the Fifth Directorate.

For technical reasons, we regret to say we must cancel the operation planned by our two services.

Sincerely,
SERGEI TRETYAKOV,
Colonel, Federal Security Service

Hathaway cursed under his breath, then called his secretary.

"Find Jeff for me."

When Jeff Soloway came in, the FBI chief silently handed him the message.

"Jesus, this is crappy!" exclaimed the agent. "Think we can make them change their minds?"

"No. If that were the case, Tretyakov would've phoned, not sent an email."

"But why?"

Hathaway shrugged.

"We'll find out someday. Or maybe not. That's the way it is with Russians."

"So what do we do?"

"We shut everything down. Send Amritzar home. Back in the United States, we can try to set him up with a Stinger or an old blue-pipe missile. Maybe a French Mistral; we have a few of them. So tell your Pakistani boy he has to go home."

"I better get the two hundred thousand dollars back, too," said Soloway. "That's bureau money."

"I know. You signed for it."

Soloway called Amritzar's cell phone for the tenth time, but it went straight to voice mail. He finally elected to leave a message, asking him to call back urgently.

He had barely hung up when a beep announced an incoming text. When he read it, he practically had a heart attack. The message from Amritzar's cell phone had been sent three hours earlier and been delayed, for some reason. It was very brief:

Thanks. I'm going to the meeting with your friend. I hope you will be there.

The FBI agent thought his head would explode. The delayed message suggested that Amritzar had been contacted by somebody using Soloway's name, and had gone to take delivery of the missile.

He sprinted to Hathaway's office.

"I have to see the boss," he told the secretary. "It's an emergency."

Two minutes later he was with Hathaway. It didn't take the FBI chief long to figure out what had happened.

"My God! The Russkis have fucked us! We have to find Amritzar, at any cost."

"He's not answering his cell phone."

"Go stake out his hotel and don't budge. He's either there, or he'll come back."

Soloway was working on his fifth espresso. He was sprawled on a bench in the Belgrade lobby, his eyes locked on the front door.

When he first arrived, he had phoned the Amritzars' room. Benazir answered and told him that her husband hadn't come in yet.

Soloway dialed the cell phone number again, with no better result. He felt helpless.

He could feel himself shrinking by the moment. The way it looked, the Russians had pulled a dirty trick on them, God knows why.

And now Amritzar was somewhere out there with a sophisticated surface-to-air missile, planning to shoot down the U.S. president's plane, which was due in a week.

It was enough to make you tear your hair out.

If they didn't get their hands on him, it would be a disaster.

CHAPTER
15

Malko looked at his watch. It was exactly seven o'clock, and Julia Naryshkin was due any minute. He planned to take her to Café Pushkin. What happened after that would depend on her.

The day had passed slowly, with Malko wondering if the FBI had wrapped up its operation. He hadn't heard any news.

His cell rang, and when Malko saw who was calling, his pulse speeded up. She must be calling to cancel, he thought.

"Hi, it's Julia," said the young woman smoothly. "I have a little problem."

"What's that?" asked Malko, who was sure he knew what she was going to say.

"My car broke down and I can't find a taxi. Would you mind coming out to my place?"

Malko practically kissed the phone.

"With pleasure," he said. "Just give me the address. But it's going to take me a good half hour to get there."

"No problem," she said lightly. "It'll give me time to fix

us something to eat. As you know, I'm in Peredelkino, about five miles beyond the MKAD. I live in a big *izba*, in Apartment Six. Ring the bell and I'll let you in. If you get lost, call me."

Malko was already in the elevator.

Night had long since fallen, and Jeff Soloway had a crick in his neck from scanning the Hotel Belgrade entrance. Benazir Amritzar was still up in Room 807, and her husband still hadn't returned.

The FBI agent stepped out to Smolenskaya Street and phoned his boss. Bruce Hathaway answered immediately.

"Is he back yet?"

"No."

A heavy silence followed, then Hathaway said:

"I'm sending you a car and backup. We can't abandon the stakeout, and there's no way you can spend the night in the lobby."

Hathaway decided to wait until the next day before raising the alarm in D.C. He was fully aware that the consequences for the White House might be catastrophic.

Malko's taxi made good time and soon passed the MKAD Ring Road. It slowed as they approached Peredelkino, and Malko spotted a big wooden building strung with Christmas lights on his left.

"It's over there," he told the driver.

Malko paid him 2,500 rubles and got out. A spotlight lit up the *izba*'s porch and front door. He rang the bell for number 6, and Julia's melodious voice answered on the intercom.

"I'll buzz you in," she said. "My apartment is at the end of the hallway, facing you."

The place smelled of pinewood and fresh paint. Julia was standing on her threshold, framed in a rectangle of light. As he got close, Malko noticed she was wearing perfume, which few Russian women did. She stepped aside to let him in, and their eyes met.

"It was nice of you to come out here," she said. "It's a long way."

She was wearing a long black skirt with a wide belt, high heels, and a black blouse that molded to her breasts, which were unconfined by a bra, as before. Except for a touch of blue under her eyes, she wore no makeup.

Julia's apartment was very cozy, with paintings, carpets, and lamps everywhere. A wooden staircase led up to a loft.

She took him into the kitchen, where she'd set out plates of food: herring, pickles, smoked salmon, salad, and *zakuski*, along with a bottle of Tsarskaya.

Julia opened the vodka, poured two glasses, and handed one to Malko.

"Welcome," she said.

They clinked glasses, and he tossed his vodka down at a gulp.

"You drink like a Russian! Better take it easy."

Her comment could have two meanings, and Malko

didn't know quite how to approach her. They hadn't touched, and aside from her lack of a bra, Julia was dressed very conservatively.

They sat down at the table and attacked the herring.

Soft Russian folk music filled the apartment, and no sounds could be heard from outside. It felt like a throwback to a bygone era. Julia was very attentive, putting pieces of smoked fish on Malko's plate and refilling his glass.

"Gocha told me a lot of fascinating things about you," she said. "You must have stories to tell."

She was looking at him almost hungrily.

The Tsarskaya bottle was now half-empty, and Julia's eyes were shining. Relaxed by the vodka, Malko was eager to take their relationship to the next level.

The young woman stood up and stretched.

"Come upstairs with me," she said. "I want to show you my paintings. You can tell me if you like any of them."

She started up the stairs with Malko on her heels. The loft held a kind of office with modern paintings hanging on the walls, and a big bed in the back.

Julia turned to him and said:

"Which do you like?"

Malko wasn't looking at the paintings, however, but at the young woman's chest. Once again, their eyes met. Daringly, he reached out and put his fingertips on her right breast. Feeling the nipple stiffen gave him a jolt of adrenaline. He repeated the gesture with his left hand, with the same result.

Julia didn't seem to react, but her breath came faster.

Malko moved his hands over the fabric, circling the now firm nipples. His crotch began to ache.

Leaving her breasts, Malko shifted his hands to her hips, squeezing the warm flesh. Julia immediately moved toward him, close enough to touch. As if drawn by a force field, their two bodies hurtled toward each other. The young woman's mouth landed in the crook of Malko's neck, her warm lips moving over his skin. When he seized her breasts again, she moaned.

Eyes closed, she raised her face to his. Their lips came together quite naturally. She kissed him with the delicacy of a cat, teasing him with the extraordinarily agile tip of her tongue.

Malko felt as if his cock were on fire. He pushed Julia against a desk and lifted her long skirt, revealing heavy black stockings held up by garters.

Leaning against the desk, Julia let him raise her skirt completely, revealing she was naked. When he set his finger on her swollen cunt, she moaned again and shuddered, coming immediately.

He started tearing at his clothes. The moment his cock was out, Julia grabbed and squeezed it. Leaning backward, she spread her legs and said just one word:

"Now."

She kept her eyes on his cock as he pushed against her.

But Malko had a hard time entering her. It was as if she weren't ready for him, which hardly seemed to be the case. At the same time, it almost felt illicit, which was incredibly exciting.

Julia reached down and seized his cock. She knelt and took it in her mouth quite naturally, but only for a moment. Leading Malko to the bed, she made him lie down on his back.

Then she pulled off his pants and underwear and straddled him, an eager glint in her eyes.

"I'm very tight," she murmured. "This way, you'll manage better."

Grasping his cock, she moved it to her pussy, and waited, motionless.

Malko got the message. He pushed upward, past an initial barrier. Biting her lips, Julia seemed to be in pain. But then she grew wetter, and he slipped in, inch by inch, until he couldn't go any farther. She was as tight as a virgin.

Chest upright and eyes closed, Julia was panting. She gave a little cry.

"There you go!" she said. "You're all the way in."

She seemed to get off on her own words. Then she began rocking back and forth. And gave another sharp cry.

Malko could feel her getting soft and juicy. She had just come a second time. But that apparently wasn't enough, because once again she began to sway like a metronome while Malko twisted her nipples. With another spasm, Julia came a third time, then slumped onto his chest.

"I've wanted to make love with you ever since I first laid eyes on you," she murmured. "It was like an ache in my belly. It's better now."

"Why did you want me so much?" asked Malko, smiling.

"Because I sense things about you that I like. My old lover Magomed was a brute. He mounted me like a bull and didn't care if I came or not. But he was a strong, dangerous man, like you."

As she gently stroked Malko's chest, he thought he could feel her getting wet again.

"Some other time," she said, almost with regret. "I've come enough for one night. I'll drive you back to town."

"I thought your car had broken down."

Julia gave him an angelic smile.

"I don't like having sex in hotels, and I decided I wanted you tonight."

She pulled away from him, and kissed his prick. Then she shook her head, running her fingers through her curly mane.

"Next time you can fuck me right on the desk, like a muzhik. I like that too."

"Do you always put on stockings when you want to have sex?"

She smiled.

"Gocha said you liked that. I wanted to give you something to remember me by."

———

Jeff Soloway shook himself as his vision of the Hotel Belgrade façade began to blur. He and the other FBI agent who'd brought the car had taken turns watching all night long, but Amritzar hadn't shown up.

Soloway decided to try one last time. He phoned the hotel and asked for Room 807. Benazir answered, sounding both tense and sleepy.

"Good morning. I'm looking for Parviz," he said.

"I don't know where he is," she said, "and I'm terribly worried. He hasn't come back and he hasn't phoned. He must've had an accident. I'm going to call the police. Who are you?"

"A friend of his," said Soloway, hanging up.

He turned to his partner and said:

"It's all over."

The FBI operation had turned into a nightmare. A terrorist armed with an advanced surface-to-air missile was now on the prowl and determined to shoot down the president's plane.

Rem Tolkachev gazed thoughtfully at his office door as it closed behind Alexander Bortnikov.

The FSB chief had brought over the file on the theft of the Igla-S in Kolomna and the killing of the two men transporting it. But the missile still hadn't been found.

The service had apparently followed Tolkachev's orders to the letter. In Moscow, an FSB team waited for the missile to be delivered to FBI agent Jeff Soloway and his buyer, Parviz Amritzar.

Two arrests were then supposed to be made by the FSB agents: Amritzar for arms trading, and Soloway for espionage.

Neither had happened.

Once the Kolomna FSB field office had reported the theft of the missile, the Fifth Directorate agents immediately canceled their part in the operation, as did their Moscow FSB colleagues.

As a result, neither the FBI agent nor the Pakistani American had been implicated. Soloway returned to the American embassy, and Amritzar went back to his hotel.

Since then, nothing. There was no sign of the Igla-S or the thieves. With the FBI and its Pakistani puppet out of the picture, the conclusion was simple: this was a strictly Russian affair, and Tolkachev had to find the people responsible. So he had taken the matter in hand, and started casting about for information.

He began by questioning Anatoly Kostina, the deputy head of Rosoboronexport. The general said he'd suggested they not help the FBI with its sting operation and then forgotten about the matter, since he knew the Kremlin would make the final decision.

The GRU confirmed asking the KBM factory for an Igla-S, to be shipped to a Moscow address furnished by the FSB.

From their modus operandi, Tolkachev figured that whoever stole the missile must be Chechen or Dagestani. The separatists hated Russians, which would explain why they'd shot the two truckers.

Tolkachev had to get the missile back. But beyond that, it was vital that he identify the separatists' sources within the Russian intelligence establishment.

As a last straw, Parviz Amritzar, the so-called terrorist the FBI brought to Moscow, had vanished from his hotel on the afternoon of the failed Igla-S delivery. The FSB hadn't thought to put surveillance on him, so nobody knew what had become of him.

The only consolation? Given that FBI agents were staking out the Hotel Belgrade, the Americans didn't know, either.

None of this would have especially interested Tolkachev, except that it suggested a disagreeable hypothesis.

Amritzar didn't know anyone in Moscow, yet just before he left the Belgrade he had received a phone call that probably precipitated his departure. The FSB had traced the caller's phone number to a Dagestani man from Makhachkala who had died three years earlier.

So how had the caller known about Parviz Amritzar? The most obvious answer was that he had joined up with some real terrorists connected to the Caucasus.

The ringing of his office doorbell interrupted Tolkachev's thoughts. One of the men in gray brought him a note from Colonel Tretyakov, saying that the head of the FBI had requested an urgent meeting. The FBI and the U.S. Secret Service were handling security for President Obama during his voyage in Russia and needed to coordinate procedures with the FSB.

This was becoming a matter of state, thought Tolkachev. If a Salafist *boivik* downed Air Force One with an Igla-S, it would cause a huge loss of face for the Kremlin. It would lead to a serious confrontation between Russia and the United States, and everyone would blame the Russians.

Feeling frustrated, Tolkachev promptly drafted a note for the president, to warn him of the situation. Then he lit one of his pastel-colored cigarettes, wondering how he was going to find the missile. It was the only way to solve his problems.

The mood in Bruce Hathaway's office was grim. The FBI chief was pale, and from the look on his colleagues' faces, you'd think the *Titanic* was sinking.

Benazir Amritzar had gone to 38 Petrovka Street to report her husband's mysterious disappearance, without being able to give the police a single clue.

Breaking the silence, Hathaway summed up the situation.

"Our 'terrorist' Parviz Amritzar has disappeared. Everything suggests that he was tricked by whoever stole the missile. The FSB is being tight-lipped, but I doubt they know any more than we do. So we now have one or more terrorists running around with a weapon capable of shooting down the president's plane."

Agent Jeff Soloway raised his hand.

"Is it possible that Amritzar conned us? Maybe he really did have contacts with terrorists. They could have spotted him when he was in Vienna. It might've come from there."

Hathaway nodded.

"Anything's possible," he said. "I'm going to shake up the Russians. Unless they deliberately set out to screw us, they must be seriously worried."

Hathaway fell silent, and the heavy gloom returned. Then he spoke again.

"Gentlemen, I have to draft a detailed report on this situation for the White House. It'll be up to them to take the necessary measures."

In other words, canceling the president's trip.

Hathaway said nothing more. He now had to explain

to the White House that an FBI operation had gone awry and loosed a terrorist with the most effective antiaircraft weapon currently available. It was enough to turn your hair gray.

Malko slept late, past the Kempinski's breakfast hours. An erotically satisfied Julia Naryshkin left her stamp on a man. He wondered if he shouldn't stay on in Moscow, to see her again.

But when he phoned, he got her voice mail. Better not alert Gocha, he thought. Stealing the Georgian's girlfriends was becoming a habit, and Malko wasn't sure Gocha would like it.

Before leaving, he decided to do some shopping at Eliseevsky on Tverskaya. He had just entered the famed food store and was admiring its richly decorated gilt ceiling when his cell phone rang.

"Malko?" It was Tom Polgar, sounding unusually tense.

"Yes."

"Where are you?"

"At Eliseevsky, shopping. My flight's at five."

"You aren't leaving. I want to see you at the embassy as soon as possible. If you can't get a taxi, I'll send a car." The Moscow station chief sounded panicky, which wasn't like him.

"I'm sure I'll manage," said Malko. He didn't ask any questions, just left the store and hailed a cab.

Ten minutes later he was at the embassy's north gate,

giving his name to the Marine on duty. The guard glanced at a paper in front of him and promptly said:

"You're expected, sir. We'll escort you."

Polgar looked like he was having a bad day. He carefully closed his office door before speaking.

"The bureau has really stepped in shit this time," he said.

Malko couldn't help but smile.

"That's no skin off your nose, is it?"

But the station chief shook his head, clearly upset.

"I don't mind if they screw up on their own time, but now they've put us in the hot seat. I just got a message from Langley passing on the White House's instructions. They've fucked up big-time, and we have to clean up their mess."

The document he handed Malko revealed what operation Vanguard had produced: a terrorist with an Igla-S was on the loose a week before the U.S. president's arrival.

Exactly as the Pakistani-born businessman had intended.

"Amritzar doesn't seem very dangerous," remarked Malko. "After all, the FBI created him."

Polgar gave him a pitying look.

"Created him? Are you kidding? He screwed them. You don't think he stole that Igla-S all by himself, do you? Amritzar supposedly didn't know anybody in Moscow, yet he managed to go underground. He must have accomplices here, and now they're running around with a surface-to-air missile."

"But this isn't your problem," Malko objected.

"It is now," said Polgar wearily. "The FBI is in the doghouse, and they don't have many contacts in Moscow. So the White House instructed the director to take over and track down the damn missile."

"If Amritzar has partners, they must be Caucasians," said Malko. "The Salafist groups continue to harass the Russians. A few months ago a guy blew himself up at Domodedovo Airport. He'd come from Dagestan. And it wasn't revenge, just nastiness.

"The Caucasus is one big powder keg. But if the Russians aren't able to keep a lid on it, what can the CIA do?"

Polgar looked at him somberly.

"You've already worked wonders here, Malko. You know people. It'll be a lot easier than your previous assignments, because you won't be fighting the Kremlin."

"What you want me to do?"

"Go rattle some cages. Start with Gocha Sukhumi, and then others, if you can."

The station chief walked around his desk, opened a drawer, and handed Malko a Glock 26 in an ankle holster. Then he picked up what looked like an attaché case.

"It unfolds this way and makes a shield," he explained, demonstrating. "GK makes them in France, and we bought a couple. This way, you'll have some protection."

Polgar handed over the case.

"Better get going right away," he said. "This is an emergency."

"What about you?" asked Malko. "What will you be doing?"

"I'll talk to some of my counterparts. I know an FSB colonel who might tell me something."

"All right, I'll tackle Gocha."

In a way, Malko wasn't too unhappy about staying in Moscow. He still had Julia's taste in his mouth. But Polgar had given him a mission impossible.

"I was going to call you, to come have dinner this evening with Julia and me at the Turandot," said Sukhumi. The Turandot was an over-the-top restaurant where the waiters dressed like eighteenth-century valets. It was next to Café Pushkin on Tverskoy Boulevard. "And I want to talk to you about something."

"Can I see you now?" asked Malko.

"Sure, come on over. I'm at home."

While waiting for a taxi, Malko phoned Julia.

"You're coming into Moscow this evening."

"How do you know that?"

"From Gocha. Can I see you beforehand?"

"You're insatiable!" the young woman said with a throaty laugh. "But I don't like to get my wires crossed. Can't you wait until tomorrow?"

She's got a hell of a nerve, thought Malko, since she was planning to spend the night with Gocha! Aloud he said:

"I want to see you for another reason. It'll amuse you."

"All right," she said after a brief hesitation. "Let's meet at the Kalina bar at six. Nobody knows me there."

Thirty seconds later, Malko was on his way to the House on the Embankment.

Arzo Khadjiev had just finished rolling each of the eight missiles in carpets, and you'd have to look closely to spot the trick. He walked over to Amritzar's corpse, which was wrapped in plastic sheeting, and sniffed. Luckily, it didn't smell.

Not yet, anyway.

Now all Khadjiev had to do was to wait for the green light to load the missiles in a truck and head for Makhach-kala. The trip would earn him $20,000, enough to buy another wife.

A devout Muslim and a follower of Wahla Arsaiev, Khadjiev prayed five times a day and considered killing infidels to be a sacred duty. He also believed that while awaiting the *houris* promised to martyrs in paradise, a good Muslim should have several wives.

Khadjiev nursed a deep hatred for Russians, and with good reason. A Spetsnaz had once mangled his ten-year-old brother's legs with a burst of AK-47 fire. He'd been trying to force their mother to reveal the hiding place of big brother Arzo, who had joined the *boiviki*. When fighting in Chechnya, Khadjiev relished decapitating Russian prisoners. Today he dreamed of the day when one of the Igla-S missiles would bring down a Russian plane or helicopter.

———

Malko found Sukhumi in his little office, busy taking bundles of five-thousand-ruble notes from a cardboard box. He counted them, then handed them to his maid Nadia, who stacked them in a safe big enough to hide a corpse.

"Hi, there!" said Sukhumi. "I'm almost done."

Malko refrained from asking him if he'd just won the lottery. Between two bundles, Nadia gave Malko a suggestive look. She enjoyed taking care of Sukhumi's friends.

With the last bundle safely stowed, they moved into the living room, where Gocha flopped down on a stained velvet sofa.

"I wanted to see you for something besides dinner," he said. "My FSB buddy gave me a tip. Some guys attacked the van carrying the Igla-S from the KBM factory to Moscow. They wasted the driver and his escort."

"Do they know who it was?" asked Malko.

"Nope. They suspect it was Caucasians, of course. But not Chechens, because Putin's little pal Kadyrov has wiped out all the *boiviki*."

"So where could they be from?"

Sukhumi made a vague gesture.

"Ingushetia, maybe, or Dagestan. That's where the Wahhabists are. The guys behind the recent attacks in Moscow were all Dagestanis."

So Tom's theory is right, thought Malko. The FBI's fake terrorist had found some real ones. Not very reassuring.

"Anything else?" he asked.

"No, except that everybody in the FSB is at battle stations." Sukhumi paused. "Okay, that's it. I'll see you at dinner, later."

The FBI had stuck its nose in a hornets' nest. If Malko couldn't find anything out, President Barack Obama would have to cancel his trip—at the cost of a diplomatic crisis.

CHAPTER 17

When Malko entered the Kalina, Julia Naryshkin was already ensconced in a booth partly hidden by the bar. Except for a lone hooker chewing gum in a corner, the café was empty.

He put his hand on her thigh, but she gently pushed it away.

"Sorry, but I don't allow public displays of affection," she said with a smile. "When we're alone, you can do whatever you like. If you're still interested, that is."

She looked him over.

"So what did you want to ask me?"

After ordering a vodka to go with Julia's tea, Malko began cautiously.

"Has Gocha told you what I do for a living?"

"Of course. Otherwise, why would I spread my legs for you? I choose what I put in my body."

Malko let that go without comment, and continued.

"Do you know Dagestan well?"

"Well, sure. I almost converted to Islam there. And the president tried to kill Magomed to get me into bed."

"Which is what he did," said Malko. "Your friend was . . ."

"The Dagestanis are brutal," Julia said with an easy smile. "When the attack failed, Magomed passed the word that if the president kidnapped me, he would kill every member of his family, near and far, including their pets and animals. And that wasn't just talk.

"What else would you like to know?"

"A terrorist group has stolen a surface-to-air missile near Moscow and is preparing an attack. They're probably Dagestani. Do you have any idea how to find them?"

Julia burst out laughing.

"If I knew that, I would be the head of the FSB, and Putin would have awarded me the Order of the Red Star! Anyway, that kind of attack isn't your problem; it's the FSB's."

"The situation's a little more complicated than I've described, Julia. Can you point me to someone who knows the Dagestanis in Moscow?"

"There's an important imam who heads a little mosque on Tatarskaya Street. A lot of Dagestanis go to see him. But I think he's an FSB informer."

Malko smiled patiently.

"Those aren't the kind of people I'm interested in, as you know perfectly well."

Julia sipped her tea, then set her cup down and said:

"I know a woman who knows a lot of Dagestanis, Marina Pirogoska. She's a *bliat*"—a prostitute.

"Is she Dagestani?"

"No, she's Russian. She hangs out at Hot Dog's, a pickup bar on the Zemlyanoy Val section of the Garden Ring."

"How do you know her?"

"I met her with Magomed. He came to Moscow with a young cousin who was looking for work here. Some Dagestanis said Marina might help him."

"Why?"

"She's not just a hooker. She owns a couple of cars, mainly old Lada 1500s, and she rents them out to Dagestanis by the day as gypsy cabs. We spent some time with her at the bar that evening, and left Magomed's cousin with her."

"Do you think she's connected with terrorists?"

Julia couldn't help but smile.

"In Dagestan everybody is somebody's cousin, more or less, or their brother-in-law, or a member of the same clan or extended family. Among all those people, of course there are terrorists.

"Except that in Dagestan it's not quite the same thing. Everyone commits extortion, kidnapping, and murder. Makhachkala must be the only capital in the world where children go to school in armored Mercedes."

She glanced at her watch.

"Okay, it's time for me to meet Gocha. When I'm late, he gets as jealous as a tiger." She paused. "If you approach Marina, be very careful. I'm sure she's only alive because she has a powerful *kricha*. Otherwise one of her drivers would've slit her throat instead of returning her Lada."

They left the restaurant together, and Malko accompanied Julia to her Austin Cooper, which was parked on a side street.

On Novy Arbat, a taxi stopped the moment he raised his arm.

"The American embassy," he told the driver. "I'll give you three hundred rubles."

Tom Polgar was going to be pleased.

Anna Polikovska was looking exceptionally sexy this evening, with a red blouse tight across her large breasts and a short, dark skirt over black stockings.

Alexei Somov was late, as usual, and Anna had already drunk two vodkas.

Several men had been circling around, assuming she was a prostitute. The Metropol bar was alive with sexy companionship, available by the hour.

Finally, Somov's tall figure emerged from the gloom. Seeing Anna's outfit, he licked his lips. He plopped down in a nearby chair and put his hand on her black-stockinged thigh, but she wriggled away, laughing.

"Wait! I've got something funny to tell you."

"Yeah, what?"

"Tretyakov got a royal chewing-out by his boss Alexander Bortnikov today! The colonel is the one who ordered the Igla-S shipped from Kolomna, so he's in hot water. He's sending some FSB investigators down there tomorrow, to try to find out what happened."

Somov froze in his seat. Anatoly Molov, the man who

agreed to release eight missiles while listing only one on the books, was a longtime friend, and had served him loyally in Chechnya. A man who wouldn't talk.

Except that he knew the FSB's methods. After they'd ripped Molov's fingernails out and drilled his teeth, he might be less loyal—and more talkative.

When the FSB was motivated, it could be pretty ferocious.

Molov now represented a clear and present danger.

"What's the matter with you?" asked Anna.

Somov had taken his hand off her thigh and was staring into space.

"Nothing," he said. "But I can't stay."

"You're kidding!"

He managed a smile.

"It's just a rain delay, *zaika maya*."

Somov's mind was racing. The FSB action meant he had to take some precautions.

First, get the missiles out of Moscow right away and wrap up the operation. Then eliminate anything that would link him to the affair. Fortunately, there was no written evidence of his involvement. And except for Anna, nothing else connected him to it.

He leaned over and kissed her lightly, fondling her breast.

"We'll party tomorrow," he promised. "Tonight, I have some problems I have to deal with."

———

Under a fine rain, Malko's taxi cruised slowly along the Garden Ring's inner sidewalk. The driver didn't know where Hot Dog's was, and they had practically circled the whole city.

Suddenly a cement building hung with strings of lights came into view. A couple of taxis were parked at the curb, and a ramp led up to a black door.

"That must be it," said the driver.

They were in the Taganka district, near the Moskva River.

Malko walked up the ramp to the entrance and opened the door, to find a box office on his right displaying the entrance fee: three hundred rubles.

Deafening music spilled from a shadowy interior. He paid, and ran into a pair of bouncers. They had suspicious eyes and were built like gorillas. They ran a handheld explosives detector over his body before letting him in.

Malko thanked his lucky stars he'd left the Glock behind at the Kempinski.

The club had a low ceiling, and was empty aside from a few customers along a big L-shaped bar. Two men were glued to a soccer game on the television while a trio of women sipped sodas sadly. Malko slipped in among them and ordered a beer. It wasn't smart to drink the vodka in a place like this; it could make you blind.

The girls were giving him sidelong looks, and after a moment one of them came closer.

"*Vui gavarite po russky?*" she asked.

"*Da, gavaryu,*" Malko said with a smile.

He bought the woman a beer, and they started the kind of conversation you have in bars.

She wasn't bad-looking. A well-dressed brunette, nice face, big mouth.

"What's your name?" he asked.

"Marina. What's yours?"

"Malko," he said, his pulse speeding up. Luck really is on my side tonight, he thought. The woman quickly sensed his interest.

"Want to go back to your place?" she asked quietly. "It's only sixteen hundred rubles."

She made her proposition very naturally.

"I can't tonight," he said. "But maybe tomorrow."

Marina didn't argue. But when he finished his beer and got down from his stool, she asked:

"Need a taxi?"

Malko pretended to be surprised.

"Do you drive a cab?"

She burst out laughing.

"No, but I own a couple of cars and rent them to Caucasians as gypsy cabs. They charge less than a regular taxi."

"Isn't it dangerous?" asked Malko. "Caucasians have a bad reputation."

"Mine are very sweet," she said. "Want to see the car? It's right outside."

Malko followed her out. By the light of an electric utility lamp, a young, dark-skinned man was fiddling under the hood of an old maroon Lada parked below the ramp.

Marina called to him.

"Javatkhan!"

When the man raised his head, he looked wild: unshaven, deep-set eyes, sharp features.

"You're going to drive this gentleman to his hotel," she ordered.

"All right." He got behind the wheel.

Marina came close to Malko.

"I'll be here tomorrow, around the same time," she said. Then she added, "Don't give him more than four hundred rubles."

The Lada's seat sagged and its shocks were shot, but Malko didn't regret coming to Hot Dog's. At last he had a lead to follow.

Alexei Somov checked the time on his solid gold Rolex, which he'd traded for a crate of ammunition back in the Caucasus. The man who gave it to him got it off an international official kidnapped by the *boiviki*. His family had refused to pay a ransom, so they eventually cut his throat.

"I'll be here at five tomorrow morning, Arzo," he said. "I'll leave my car in the courtyard."

"Okay."

Somov got back behind the wheel of his Mercedes. Having taken these first necessary steps, he breathed easier.

His urge for sex came rushing back, too. I bet Marina's at Hot Dog's now, he thought. She was mainly a whore, but she was a smart one, and she fucked so well you forgot about that. If she wasn't there, he would settle for having one of her girlfriends suck him off.

Somov had gotten to know Marina by accident, after spending a night with her. Then, when he learned about her car business, he started using her Dagestanis for occasional errands. In exchange, he gave her protection. She needed it, because some of her guys were real animals.

A half hour later, he pulled up in front of Hot Dog's. The two bouncers stepped back respectfully. Somov could strangle one in each hand, and they knew it. In Russia, people admired physical strength.

By a miracle, Marina was at the bar, chatting with an expat. Somov sat down on the stool behind her and wrapped his big hand around her butt. She whipped around, furious, but immediately relaxed when she recognized him.

"Alexei Ivanovich!"

Seeing this Russian bear, the expat beat a cautious retreat.

Somov whispered into Marina's ear.

"I feel like fucking your brains out, *dushenka*."

"Anytime you like," she purred. "I can almost feel you inside me."

She slid off the bar stool, and they left. The bartender wisely didn't complain that she hadn't paid for her drink.

They were barely in the Mercedes before Marina snuggled up to Somov and started to unzip his pants.

"I want you to be as stiff as a Kalashnikov barrel when we get there."

She promptly bent to her task, and Somov soon found he was having trouble driving.

"Cut that out! If the highway patrol stops us, they'll give us a hard time."

Marina straightened up, but kept her little hand wrapped around her lover's cock.

"By the way, I have a new taxi customer," she said. "A foreigner."

"Oh, really?" said Somov indifferently.

"He needs to get around Moscow. He speaks Russian. Javatkhan dropped him off at the Kempinski. Good-looking, too; tall, blond, elegant."

"Son of a bitch!" Somov muttered under his breath, so quietly she barely heard him.

Somov didn't believe in coincidences. This could only be the CIA agent that the FSB had noticed. How had he managed to find Marina? In any case, Somov had to cut the connection right away. It was a mortal danger. He heaved a sigh. No doubt about it: even the best laid plans hid unpleasant surprises.

He remembered the proverb that Stalin liked to quote: "No man, no problem."

He had to put it in action as soon as possible.

CHAPTER

18

The streets of Kolomna weren't yet very busy
when Arzo Khadjiev swung onto Leninsky Avenue.

"Turn right," said Alexei Somov a few moments later.

They took a small road lined by fifteen-story apartment blocks. On the outskirts of town, they drove over
train tracks on a level crossing. A hundred yards farther,
Somov had Khadjiev stop the car in front of a decrepit,
yellowish three-story building. Somov turned and said:

"Give me your thing."

The Dagestani pulled the Makarov with the long
silencer from his belt and handed it to him.

"Turn the car around, and be ready to leave," ordered
Somov. "This won't take long."

He strode toward the building. It was seven thirty in
the morning. Anatoly Molov started work at KBM at
eight, so he should be up and dressed. Somov punched
an access code into the building's keypad.

Molov lived on the second floor. There was no elevator, so Somov took the stairs.

He pressed the doorbell and heard steps from inside the apartment.

"Who's there?" came a man's voice.

"It's me, Alexei Ivanovich."

The door opened immediately. As expected, the KBM manager was dressed and ready to leave for work. He looked at Somov in surprise.

"What's going on?" he asked. "Why didn't you call? I could have already left."

"I need to talk with you."

Molov stepped aside and said, "Come on in."

Preceding Somov into the living room, Molov didn't see his visitor take out the pistol. Somov brought the end of the silencer close to Molov's neck and pulled the trigger. The detonation was so faint, it wouldn't even be heard through the door. Molov staggered forward and fell, first to his knees, then flat on his face. Somov carefully fired a second bullet in Molov's head, pocketed the pistol, and headed for the door.

When he climbed in next to Khadjiev, not five minutes had passed, and they hadn't seen a soul.

"Let's go," said Somov. "We're going back to Moscow."

He relaxed only when they were on the M5.

"Tonight you'll be the one doing the work."

That meant killing a man who was getting too close to the one person who might give Somov away.

The four FSB agents showed up at the KBM factory at exactly eight o'clock. The plant manager, Ivan Babichev, welcomed them and made them comfortable in his office.

"Anatoly Molov handles our inventory, but he's late today," Babichev said. "I'll call him."

Which he did.

"He's not answering. He must be on his way."

After drinking some more tea, the FSB agents began to get impatient.

"Why don't we start without him?" one suggested.

Babichev led them to the warehouse area, and an employee gave them the delivery and shipment logbook. Igla missiles lay in various stages of fabrication on a nearby assembly line.

The agents got to work checking the inventory records, and Babichev went back to his office.

He enjoyed a quiet morning of work until just before lunchtime, when one of the FSB investigators came into his office.

"Gospodin Babichev, we've uncovered a serious discrepancy," he said. "According to your books it's not just one Igla-S that's missing, but eight of them!"

Babichev could hardly believe his ears.

"Did you discuss this with Anatoly Nikolayevich?"

"He still hasn't arrived."

"He must be sick," said the manager. "I'll send somebody to his place."

"Don't bother. Give us someone to show us the way, and we'll go ourselves."

As Colonel Tretyakov listened to the report from the team he'd sent to Kolomna, he could feel the blood draining from his face.

"*Eight* missiles gone?" he spat. "And the inventory manager killed?"

"Two bullets to the head," said the FSB agent. "The local *politsiya* is investigating."

"I have to tell the chief right away."

When Tretyakov hung up a few minutes later, he was in shock. This whole thing was much more serious than he'd imagined. It was now a full-scale terrorist plot, and it could only come from the Caucasus. Just thinking of what criminally minded people could do with those missiles gave him cold sweats. Every day, hundreds of civilian planes took off or landed at Moscow. Securing airports was a monumental task, and if just one Russian passenger plane were shot down, it would traumatize the whole country.

He called his secretary.

"Anna, have a team go to the Hotel Belgrade and bring Parviz Amritzar's wife here."

He couldn't afford to overlook any trail. Maybe the FBI had made a mistake with Amritzar. Whoever had managed to steal eight missiles and commit three murders was no amateur.

"I'll see you at Café Pushkin in an hour," Gocha announced.

Malko was about to leave for the embassy to report on his meeting with Marina, but he figured Sukhumi was probably calling him for more than just lunch.

When he reached the restaurant, Gocha was at the bar.

"I don't have time to eat," said the Georgian. "But I just heard something that'll blow your mind."

When Sukhumi described what the FSB learned in Kolomna, Malko was open-mouthed. They were far from the innocent FBI sting. Along the way, something had gone seriously wrong. The seemingly naïve Amritzar had turned around and screwed his FBI handlers. He had made contact with terrorists in Moscow with inside connections, and they had stolen the missiles.

"What is the FSB saying?" he asked.

"They're in a complete panic. They don't understand what's happening. There was nothing special about the guy who inventoried the missiles. He was killed to keep him from talking. Which means the terrorists were tipped off to the FSB agents' visit to Kolomna ahead of time.

"I think you better drop this, Malko. It's a strictly Russian affair now. The FBI isn't involved anymore."

"Thanks, Gocha. I'll think about it."

Sukhumi apparently didn't know what Julia had told him about Dagestanis, or about Marina and her taxis—though they could well have nothing to do with any of this.

After polishing off some herring and a couple of vodkas, Malko left Gocha and headed for the embassy.

"My God!" cried Tom Polgar. "That's incredible! I've got to alert Langley immediately."

The FBI sting had sparked a potential disaster. Because if someone had stolen the missiles, they must be planning to use them. . . .

"What else have you learned?"

Malko described his meeting with Marina Pirogoska, then said:

"It may have no connection with the missile business, and at this point I think we ought to back away from the whole thing. It would be nice to warn the FSB that a Caucasian network might be operating through this woman. They have better ways to get at the truth than we do. And they might see us as meddling in their affairs."

"Sorry, Malko, but I don't agree," said Polgar, shaking his head. "You have a trail, follow it. We may learn something interesting. These terrorists obviously have accomplices in the intelligence services. If we find out who they are, we'll have a major bargaining chip to use down the road. So stay on the case."

Malko was on his way back to the Kempinski when his cell phone beeped.

"I'm in Moscow with nothing to do until dinnertime," came Julia's lilting voice. "We could have a drink."

"Come to the Kempinski."

"You know I don't much like hotels," she said. "Why don't you meet me at Aist instead? It's a café on Malaya Bronnaya Street, in the Patriarch's Ponds district. It's quiet and they serve all kinds of teas."

She hung up before Malko had time to argue, leaving him no choice but to change his itinerary.

When his taxi pulled up at the Aist, Malko saw a floodlit building set among trees decorated with strings of lights. A statue of two dancing storks stood in a patch of gravel near the entrance. The Patriarch's Ponds area was one of the most exclusive parts of Moscow, and the Aist was ostentatiously elegant.

Chauffeurs with shaved heads lounged against the many Mercedes with tinted windows double-parked nearby.

Julia was seated in a booth at the back, looking very self-possessed. She was the only woman in the place.

Malko had to walk a gauntlet of tables of tough-looking guys with mustaches looking at him curiously.

He slid in next to the young woman and smiled at her.

"We would've been more comfortable at the Kempinski."

"Hey, I like this place," she said. "It's where rich Dagestanis go when they're in town. I used to come here a lot when I was with Magomed."

"So this is a pilgrimage?"

"People don't bother single women here. There's practically only Caucasians. See that table with four men near the entrance? That's the mayor of Makhachkala and the airport director. Wealthy, dangerous people. They're distant cousins of Magomed. If somebody bothered me, they would kill him. I'm like a part of their family.

"If you ever have problems in Dagestan, these are the people you'll have to deal with."

"Aside from your friend Marina, I don't have anything to do with any Dagestanis," Malko assured her.

"Did she turn out to be helpful?"

"Maybe. I don't know yet."

"Keep me posted."

"When can we see each other again?"

Julia seemed to think this over, then said:

"Tomorrow. Gocha is going to Yekaterinburg."

She was being almost faithful, which Malko found irritating.

"Are you in love with him?"

"No, but he's exciting," she explained. "And he's in love with me. Does that bother you?"

The arrival of a waiter with pots of tea prevented him from answering. Julia was being both distant and provocative. When their eyes met, Malko promised himself to take revenge the next time they made love.

Just then, two youngish men in leather coats entered the restaurant. They had long hair, weathered faces, and neatly trimmed beards. They chatted with the four men sitting near the entrance, then took a long look at Julia and Malko's table.

Suddenly one of them walked over, and Julia stiffened. Malko saw her hand tighten on the tablecloth. The man stopped in front of them, and stared first at Malko, then Julia.

Reaching into his coat pocket, he took out something round and black, set it on the table, and walked away.

Malko's heart thudded in his chest.

It was a grenade!

Then he realized that the pin hadn't been pulled. It wasn't going to explode.

"What the hell's that supposed to mean?" he snapped.

Julia looked upset.

"That was Karon, Magomed's cousin. As he sees it, I still belong to his cousin, and he wanted to remind me of that. What he did is pretty common in Dagestan. Everybody there walks around with grenades like this one in their pockets. It's a Diakonov 33; it doesn't do much collateral damage.

"Karon didn't mean any harm. Moscow is civilized territory. In Dagestan he might have killed you."

She had picked up the grenade and held it out to Malko.

"Here, take it."

He slipped it into his coat pocket.

"Throw it down a sewer," she suggested. "I shouldn't have come here with you. I'm very sorry."

Malko was calling to the waiter.

"The check, please."

"I don't have much time," she said.

As they made for the exit, the four Caucasians at the table gave them long, unfriendly looks.

When Malko told the cabdriver to take them to the Kempinski, Julia didn't object.

Malko didn't even have time to take the grenade from his coat pocket. The moment they were in his suite in the Kempinski, Julia threw herself into his arms, as if asking for forgiveness. He twisted her curly red hair into a ponytail and pulled her head back.

"You know what you have to do now, don't you?" he said, looking her in the eye.

After a brief moment of hesitant defiance, her gaze softened. She smoothly sank to her knees onto the thick carpet in front of Malko. Like an obedient courtesan, she unzipped his trousers, reached around his underpants for his cock, and took it in her mouth.

Leaning against the sofa and gazing at the Kremlin through the bay window, Malko felt her warm mouth enveloping him.

She clearly wanted to be forgiven.

Gripping the ponytail, he guided her head back and forth, in and out. It felt wonderful.

It was like training a horse, that moment when a willful animal suddenly starts to obey you. Until now, Julia Naryshkin had hardly behaved like an obedient woman. Now she was giving him a magisterial blow job, taking him as deep in her throat as she could, her eyes closed.

She was so skillful that Malko soon felt his orgasm rising, and forced himself even deeper into her mouth.

She tried to pull away, but he grabbed her by the neck

and yanked her close. A moment later, he came. She almost gagged, but swallowed anyway, even though he had released her head.

Julia stood and faced him then, her eyes moist. She was still wearing her coat and the blouse that showed off her nipples. She put her right hand under her skirt for a moment and pulled a scrap of black lace down her leg.

Her panties.

Leaning back on the sofa, she lifted the long skirt up over her hips, revealing a reddish, well-tended bush. Malko was approaching her when the room telephone rang, and he picked it up.

"This is Ghazi-Mohammed," said a man's voice in Russian with a rough Caucasian accent. "Gospozha Marina wants to see you. She sent me to pick you up."

The night before, Malko had given his room number to the driver who'd brought him to the Kempinski. So Marina wasn't dropping him. The timing was good, because he might be able to follow the Dagestani trail through her.

"All right," he said. "I'm coming down."

He zipped his pants and faced Julia.

"I'm really sorry," he said. "This is business. Besides, you said you didn't have much time."

If looks could kill, Malko would have died on the spot.

"You're treating me like a whore!" she hissed, slowly straightening her skirt.

As he went out and closed the door, he could almost feel the woman's laser-like gaze burning into his back.

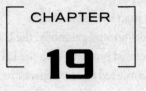
Downstairs, a purple Lada double-parked to the right of the Kempinski entrance awaited him. The driver was a young Caucasian with large, dark eyes and dirty hair. A few whiskers sprouted from his narrow chin. It wasn't the same man who had driven Malko the night before.

"Good evening, gospodin," he said with a guttural accent. "Gospozha Marina is expecting you."

Malko got in the backseat and the car took off along Raushkaya Embankment. A little later they crossed the Moskva, heading for the Garden Ring. They reached the Taganka district but passed Hot Dog's and continued on the ring road.

"Where are we going?" asked Malko.

"Home."

With the usual tie-ups, traffic was slow. About a mile farther the driver turned off the ring road, heading toward the Kursky railroad station through a shabby area with vacant lots and few lights. Marina clearly didn't live in a fancy neighborhood.

Suddenly the car sputtered, stopped, then started again. The driver cursed.

"What's the matter?" asked Malko.

"Damned fuel pump," grumbled the Caucasian.

It was a perennial problem with the Lada 1500. In the old days, Russians used to carry spare fuel filters in their wallets.

The car started sputtering again, and the driver slowed, pulling over at an empty lot.

For some reason, Malko felt ill at ease. The driver had switched on the dome light, and when Malko caught his eye in the rearview mirror, he immediately sensed he was in danger.

The car hit a rock as it slowed, and the impact threw Malko forward, giving him a glimpse of the front seat. An open newspaper had fallen to the floor, revealing a big pistol with a silencer.

He leaned back in his seat, unsure whether the driver realized he'd seen the gun. His brain was whirling. The car came to a stop just inside the lot. A perfect place for an ambush.

He watched as the man reached across the seat. All he had to do was to grab the gun, turn around, and shoot Malko at point-blank range.

And Malko had once again left the Glock 26 back at the hotel.

But he wasn't completely defenseless, he suddenly realized. Taking the grenade Julia gave him from his coat pocket, he pulled the pin and tossed it toward the driver. Then he yanked his door open and dove out.

He was flat on his stomach when a dull explosion and burst of flame erupted behind him. The car's doors were violently blasted open and its windows shattered. The interior started to burn.

Malko looked up. The driver's body hung partway out of the car. The grenade had exploded in his lap, gutting him. His mouth was open, and his chest and belly were a single bloody mass.

Red flames were starting to lick at the car's bodywork. Malko was about to leave when the flickering light illuminated a shiny black object on the ground next to the car. A cell phone. Malko stuffed it in his pocket and ran toward the train station. When he turned to look back, the Lada was ablaze. Fortunately, the street was deserted.

Sighting the Kurskaya metro station, he sprinted for it. He bought a ticket, went down to the platform, and boarded a train that left moments later.

As it rumbled toward Teatralnaya, the next station on the Number 3 line, Malko examined the phone he'd found near the Lada.

It was a Nokia. When he switched it on, a photo of a smiling young brunette in a head scarf appeared onscreen.

It took Malko a moment to recognize her: it was Benazir Amritzar! He had somehow retrieved her husband's cell phone from the dead killer.

When Malko emerged from the Teatralnaya station near the Duma, his head was buzzing with questions. Why would Amritzar give the unknown Caucasian his cell phone? And why had that man tried to kill him?

Only Marina could have sent the driver, so she had to be connected to the missile business. But Malko didn't know anything beyond what Sukhumi had told him.

It didn't take him more than half a minute to flag down a cab. The driver, a fat, cheerful woman, was delighted to earn five hundred rubles to take him to the Kempinski.

He now had an urgent task: find Marina, if she hadn't disappeared. It would be interesting to see how she reacted to seeing him.

Parked on Lesnaya Street across from the wholesale fruit store, Somov had been waiting in his Mercedes for almost an hour. Arzo should have returned long ago, he thought.

Somov's orders had been clear: kill the CIA agent, dump his body in a vacant lot, and come back to drive the truck with the missiles to Dagestan.

Marina had provided some extra drivers who didn't know what they was carrying. Somov was careful to keep things compartmentalized.

He'd decided to have Linge killed when he started getting too interested in Marina. He figured he wouldn't be suspicious when Khadjiev phoned him, pretending to be one of her drivers.

But something had gone wrong.

Khadjiev wasn't there, and he wasn't answering his phone.

Somov looked at his watch. He couldn't hang around forever. He would come back tomorrow to arrange the shipment of the Iglas to Dagestan, though doing that without Khadjiev might be a hassle.

As he started his Mercedes, Somov was struck by an unpleasant thought. What if Malko Linge was still alive, and he went to talk to Marina?

She didn't know anything, of course, but that could be worrisome.

Feeling tense, Malko stepped into Hot Dog's. It was late—the murder attempt had been five hours earlier—so he wasn't likely to find Marina still there. Unless she thought he was dead.

As before, the two apelike bouncers checked him out carefully. He paid his three hundred rubles and made for the bar. There were more people than the night before, and some of the tables were occupied. The crowded bar included a woman in a red jacket with long black hair sitting alone in front of a Martini Bianco on the rocks.

Malko's pulse started to race: it had to be Marina!

He came up behind her, and a sixth sense made her turn around. She was carefully made up, and he could make out slightly sagging breasts under a sheer black blouse.

"Malko!" she cried, giving him a warm smile. "I'd given up hoping you were coming."

"Why so?"

"My driver went to pick you up earlier, but you'd already left the hotel."

She radiated sincerity, and her gaze was completely open. Malko took a stool next to hers and ordered a beer.

Marina clearly hadn't sent the killer, yet she was the only person who knew the circumstances that made the ambush possible.

"Something came up," he said. "But here I am, as you see."

She gave him a flirtatious look.

"So much the better! Even if you didn't use my driver, I'm very happy to see you."

A heavy hint.

Marina now seemed eager to leave. She polished off her Martini at a gulp, leaving only the ice cubes.

"Do you have time tonight?" she asked, almost shyly.

Malko was about to say no, but thought better of it. After all, the young woman must know something.

"Sure," he said. "Let's go."

Out on the sidewalk, it was drizzling.

She opened the door of a Lada with peeling red paint. Malko's driver from the night before got behind the wheel.

"Are we going to the Kempinski?" she asked.

Impressed by his luxurious suite, Marina walked over to the picture window facing the Kremlin.

"God, it's beautiful!" she said admiringly.

She turned to Malko, and added:

"You must have a lot of money."

The request couldn't be ignored. He discreetly peeled off 1,600 rubles, which she stowed in her purse. Then she took off her blouse, revealing a lacy red bra. The rest followed. Her string panty, red as well, stopped just below a long appendicitis scar. This was common among poor Russians; Soviet-era doctors were butchers.

The young woman's blue-gray eyes expressed something unexpected among whores: sincere pleasure.

She quickly pulled off her string panty, revealing that she was completely bare, Russian style.

"You're gonna fuck me good," she whispered, embracing him.

That sounded sincere as well.

She started giving Malko a blow job while expertly massaging his perineum. The groans of pleasure she produced were well worth 1,600 rubles.

When he laid Marina across the bed, she arched her back and cried out when he entered her. Her hips moved in a kind of circular dance that heightened Malko's enjoyment.

Afterward she rested on her belly for a while, before eventually standing up.

"I'm going to leave now," she said. "You must be tired."

As she got dressed, she put a business card on the night table.

"That's my cell," she said. "If you need me or a car, just call."

Malko didn't know quite what to make of her. She was a hooker with a chauffeur who rented out cars. Deeply sensual, but somehow involved with the missile affair.

This was a slim lead, and one to be handled carefully. It had already nearly cost Malko his life.

The next thing to do was to get Parviz Amritzar's cell phone to reveal its secrets, and only the technical division people at the embassy could do that.

So far, the facts that Malko had gathered didn't fit together. He had a puzzle with some major pieces missing.

Yet without realizing it, he'd already learned quite a lot.

Colonel Dmitri Voloshino, the head of the FSB investigations department at 38 Petrovka Street, read the report carefully. It detailed the discovery of a burned Lada 1500 in a vacant lot near the Kursky train station the previous evening. The car contained a man's body, his lower body shredded by some sort of explosion, possibly a grenade. The flames had burned everything, so it was impossible to identify the man, but the discovery of a 9 mm Makarov with a silencer strongly hinted at organized crime.

Voloshino ordered the serial numbers of the car and pistol traced, but didn't give it much thought. It was almost certainly a gangland settling of scores.

Just in case, he forwarded the report to the counterterrorism directorate at the Lubyanka.

Arzo Khadjiev's partners Karon and Terek had almost finished loading the eight Igla-S into the old Ural truck. They stacked the cases wrapped in their carpets up front, then filled the rest of the truck with cartons containing flat-screen televisions, computers, and electrical appliances.

It was more than a thousand miles to Dagestan, and this way, if they were stopped along the road, they could barter their way out of trouble. On their meager pay, few border guards could afford a flat-screen TV.

As they were about to leave, the two men looked at Parviz Amritzar's body. In its plastic sheeting, it had begun to swell. They didn't feel like taking it along, and no one would be looking for it, so they decided to leave it behind.

Karon, the conscientious one, took the trouble to rig a grenade booby trap underneath it. If somebody moved the body, it would explode. A harmless little joke to punish the nosy.

Just then, his cell phone rang. It was a man he knew only as "Pavel"—almost certainly a fake name—who spoke like someone used to giving orders.

"Arzo had a problem," said the man. "Don't wait for him. I'll meet you there."

Karon didn't argue. He was paid cash on the barrel-head for his services, and this trip would be no exception. In Dagestan, an Igla-S was worth its weight in gold, he knew.

He and Terek went upstairs to the courtyard, locked the basement door, and drove out toward the ring road. They would then take the M6 to Tambov and make for Volgograd. After that, it would be the Caucasus and eventually Makhachkala.

The two men were armed, but more out of habit than fear.

People knew who they were, and anyone who bothered them would pay the price.

Malko watched as Tom Polgar studied the Nokia phone, which he'd had charged. He first looked at the photo of Benazir Amritzar, then scrolled through the list of outgoing calls. Many were to the Hotel Belgrade, and one to a number in the United States. But one call appeared to have been made to a Russian cell phone.

"I'll give the phone to the Technical Division, and see what they can get out of it," said Polgar.

"Have you talked to the FBI?" asked Malko.

"They're lying low. Bruce Hathaway would only hint vaguely that they'd screwed up."

"And no news of Parviz Amritzar, I assume."

"Nope. Bruce talked to the FSB, and they claim to be in the dark. They didn't mention the eight missiles. I think they've lost interest in Amritzar, because now they've got much bigger fish to fry: a real terrorist plot."

"What about Benazir?"

"The FSB questioned her, but she wasn't able to tell them much. They told her to stay at the hotel and not to leave the country. She's an American citizen, so we sent her our vice consul. But I'm sure she doesn't know anything.

"It looks like the FBI has precipitated a catastrophe, because they didn't know Amritzar was connected to real terrorists based here. That's why he was so eager to get to Russia; he wanted to join his pals."

Malko didn't agree.

"It seems to me more likely that he was framed," he said.

"In that case, he's dead," said Polgar soberly. "When a Russian loses his cell phone, it's not a good sign."

"The man who used it and tried to kill me looked like a Caucasian," said Malko. "And Marina deals with Caucasians. That's a lot of coincidences."

Malko paused.

"I'll repeat what I suggested before: get clear of this mare's nest, tell the Russians what we know, and let me fly back to Austria."

"No way," said Polgar firmly. "We're involved whether we like it or not. They tried to kill you, so you're in somebody's way, and it wasn't the FSB or the other secret services. We've stumbled into something a lot more complicated, and we better figure it out.

"Besides, you're forgetting the most important thing. Even if Amritzar was wholly created by the FBI, he really did want to shoot down Air Force One. The president will be here in a few days, and the FBI won't be the ones to protect them."

"What about the Russians?"

"I'm sure they don't want an incident like that, but nothing says they can prevent it. Caucasians have already struck in Moscow with impunity. They've infiltrated the intelligence services and can do whatever they like. Besides, an Igla-S can reach 12,000 feet, so you never know what might happen."

"Doesn't Air Force One have electronic countermeasures?" Malko asked in surprise.

"Of course, but the Russians claim that the Igla-S can penetrate all the ones in use today. No sense in putting it to the test."

The CIA station chief had a point. The only way any of them would rest easy was to retrieve the stolen missiles.

General Razgonov had just come from a meeting on the seventh floor of the Aquarium, right below the helipad. He was feeling tense.

Per the Kremlin's order, the head of the GRU had called in all his top deputies to brief them on the Igla theft. The information was secret, but every intelligence service in the country was told to question their sources for clues to the missiles' whereabouts.

The threat against the U.S. president's plane was also covered, of course. It would be terrible for the Kremlin if the hated Caucasians made Russian intelligence look foolish in the eyes of the world. They had already done so in the Moscow theater hostage crisis in 2002 and a number of other attacks committed under the noses of the police.

As the general formerly in charge of the North Caucasus, Razgonov felt all eyes were on him. He had dealt with enough Chechens and Dagestanis to still have contacts among them. He'd been told to approach the Wahla Arsaiev group, a likely candidate for launching this kind of attack.

This was awkward for Razgonov. After all, these were his customers, handled by his friend Alexei Somov.

Back in his office, Razgonov went over the situation in his mind. All in all, it wasn't too dire. In a few days, he would be getting eight million dollars. No one could connect him to the theft of the missiles. Anatoly Molov was dead, and the Kolomna FSB hadn't found any clues to his murder.

Parviz Amritzar, the phony terrorist, was out of the way, and the truck carrying the missiles had left Moscow for Dagestan.

Somov still didn't know what had gone wrong, but was beginning to fear the worst. If Khadjiev didn't call, it meant that he was dead. That wasn't a big deal in itself, but could anyone get back to him through the young Dagestani?

He didn't see how, even after giving it a lot of thought.

Somov had had no official knowledge of the FBI sting operation that had started this whole business.

That left Marina as the only connection. The fact that he occasionally slept with her was no crime, and he had never used her in any of his operations. So there was no point in killing her, which would only cause problems.

Somov glanced at his watch. He would be seeing Anna at the end of the day. Maybe she'd heard something. Now that the Sword and Shield restaurant near FSB headquarters had closed, it was harder to glean bits of useful information.

As Colonel Tretyakov's secretary, Anna was the only

person who knew he was aware of the FBI's original request to borrow an Igla-S. And she probably didn't realize she had tipped him off.

Somov lit a cigarette and looked out the window at the gray sky. The search for the missing Iglas would give him a perfect excuse to go to Dagestan to investigate. It would allow him to collect the eight million dollars and also dispose of the missiles. That should take some of the pressure off.

By now, Rem Tolkachev was working on practically nothing but the Igla-S affair. It went far beyond an ordinary counterterrorism action. If terrorists managed to attack the American president on Russian soil, the shock would be terrible. Many heads would roll, maybe even his own.

Tolkachev went over what he knew and what he didn't.

Parviz Amritzar had disappeared, probably to go join terrorists in the Caucasus.

Eight Igla-S missiles had been stolen, something that had never happened before. In Tolkachev's eyes that meant the terrorists must be planning to strike in Moscow. After all, Chechnya was pacified, and all its *boiviki* dead. Ingushetia was quiet. The Wahhabi groups in Dagestan didn't need surface-to-air missiles except for prestige, or to sell them, probably outside of Russia. Nobody was fighting them, and Dagestan itself only dispatched a suicide bomber to Moscow from time to time so Russia wouldn't forget about it.

For the first time in his long career, Tolkachev didn't see how to solve the problem. Meanwhile, the FSB, GRU, and the FAPSI information service were sending him blizzards of reports, most of them meaningless.

Going through the stack of documents, Tolkachev came across the surveillance report on Malko Linge, and skimmed it. His idea of killing the CIA agent now seemed a long time ago. But a sentence in the report jumped out at him. Linge was having a relationship with one Julia Naryshkin, a good-looking intellectual who'd once been the girlfriend of Makhachkala's mayor.

Hm, thought Tolkachev, the Caucasus again . . .

It might be a coincidence, of course. Magomed Nabi-yev was a refugee in a wheelchair and Naryshkin was a free woman. Just the same, Tolkachev made a note to have Gocha Sukhumi questioned, to see if she still had any connections with the Caucasus.

The report also mentioned the CIA agent's twice vis-iting a pickup bar at 26 Zemlyanoy Val Street, which was a section of the Garden Ring. The second time, he'd taken a hooker back to the Kempinski.

Tolkachev paused thoughtfully, his pen in midair. Then he went to his safe, rummaged among his files, and pulled out the one on Malko Linge.

It was as thick as a phone book.

Quickly leafing through it, he learned something interesting. In Linge's various trips to Russia, he had slept with a number of women, but never with a prosti-tute.

It could be a clue.

Tolkachev drafted an urgent request for a close-up photo of the woman, to be taken without her knowledge.

As far as he knew, Linge had no official business in Moscow, so his presence was intriguing. He was up to something, but what?

Tom Polgar handed Malko a freshly decoded message from Washington. It wasn't from Langley, but the White House.

It was brief and to the point.

As the representative of the CIA in Moscow, Polgar was instructed to schedule an immediate meeting with FSB head Alexander Bortnikov, to deliver an official message.

The State Department wanted Russian intelligence to retrieve the eight Igla-S missiles stolen from the KBM factory in Kolomna before President Barack Obama's arrival in Moscow. Otherwise the American ambassador would notify the Ministry of Foreign Affairs that the visit was being postponed.

The matter was being kept at the level of the intelligence services for the moment, so as not to cause talk.

Malko handed back the message.

"Who told the White House that there were eight missiles?"

"I did," said Polgar. "I couldn't keep that to myself."

"And the Russians aren't aware that we know?"

"I don't think so."

"This is going to rock the boat, Tom. They're going to start asking themselves questions, and they may have a few for us. We have to protect Gocha."

"I'm not about to burn our sources," said the station chief. "And the decision about the president's visit isn't mine to make. The White House is really worried about an attack, and I can't blame them."

"When will you see Bortnikov?"

"As soon as I can get an appointment," said Polgar. "I don't think it'll be a long meeting."

"Have you informed the FBI?"

"No, I haven't. They're the ones who got us into this shit."

It wasn't exactly the era of good feelings.

"So what do you want of me?" asked Malko.

Polgar smiled tightly.

"You're going to have some work to do."

"Meaning what?"

"Amritzar's cell gave us an interesting lead. You know we keep files on all the important people in Russian intelligence, right?"

"Of course. So what?"

"A call was made from the phone that we wouldn't have expected. It was to a certain Alexei Somov. He's a black-market arms dealer, ex-GRU. Apparently all of Somov's operations are vetted by a former military commander in the Caucasus, General Anatoly Razgonov. The number three man at the GRU."

CHAPTER

21

Malko was stunned.

How could a former GRU officer possibly get a call from a man the FBI suspected was a terrorist? The Igla-S affair was becoming more and more murky. Malko and Polgar already knew that the FSB planned to trap the FBI. Now suddenly the GRU was on stage, but in a role they didn't understand.

"What do you make of all this, Tom?" asked Malko.

"The only possibility I see is that the phone was no longer in Amritzar's possession when it was used."

"Which means he's dead. His killer would've taken his cell and used it to call this Alexei Somov person. That suggests a connection between the GRU and the terrorists who stole the missiles. Seems hard to believe."

"You know as much as I do," said Polgar, sighing. "But remember the shadowy connections between the Russian intelligence services and the Caucasus. The FSB was suspected of manipulating the Chechens who blew up those two Moscow buildings in 1999."

Malko shook his head, as if to clear it.

"I still think the best thing to do is for us to communicate everything we know to the FSB, and let them sort it out. We certainly don't have the means to investigate the GRU."

"That's true," said Polgar, "but this telephone number is dynamite. Let's see if we can use it to our advantage. Remember, our agenda isn't the same as the Russians'. Our main goal is to locate those missiles. And here we have a lead, even if we don't yet know how to follow it."

"What do you know about Somov?"

"Not much. He was a colonel in the GRU under General Anatoly Razgonov, who commanded the North Caucasus sector. They were based in Grozny and Makhachkala. Since then, Razgonov has risen to the number three slot in the GRU."

"Is it conceivable that an officer of his rank would have dealings with terrorists?"

Polgar shrugged.

"Normally no, but this is Russia. . . ."

"I can only think of two people who might be able to help us," said Malko. "Gocha Sukhumi and Julia Naryshkin. But I'll have to handle them with kid gloves."

"Go ahead," said the CIA station chief. "I won't say anything to anyone for the time being."

Somov looked at his plane ticket for Makhachkala. He was flying on Dagestan Airlines, a domestic airline and the only one that still flew between Moscow and the Dagestani capital. He would be leaving in four days.

He was gripped by a dull anxiety. From the press, he'd gotten a general idea of what had happened to Arzo Khadjiev, who must have been the burned corpse found in a vacant lot near the Kursky train station.

Somov wondered what had gone wrong.

Khadjiev was a veteran killer, and shouldn't have had any trouble dispatching an unarmed CIA agent. But the media also mentioned a grenade being involved. CIA agents don't normally walk around with grenades in their pockets. That was more a Caucasian thing.

Though he still couldn't understand what had happened, Somov suddenly realized that with Malko Linge alive, Marina Pirogoska had become a security risk for him.

The CIA agent was sure to learn her role in all this. She didn't know anything about Somov's plans, but if she mentioned his name to Linge, it would be disastrous.

The Americans couldn't launch an investigation in Russia, but they might well pass their information to the FSB, especially if they feared an attack on the U.S. president, or wanted revenge.

And for Somov, that would be the end.

There was only one thing to do, and it pained him: kill Marina. The Moscow FSB knew Somov was her *kricha*, but they wouldn't necessarily make the connection.

It was a step he would take before leaving for Dagestan.

When Malko walked in, Sukhumi was busy writing. He
was surrounded by stacks of papers and had a bottle of
Armenian cognac near at hand.

"I've got big news!" he cried exultantly. "Julia has
agreed to marry me!"

Gocha really is a softie at heart, thought Malko.

Seeing his look of astonishment, Sukhumi explained.

"It's true that I like fucking whores, but I need a wife,
and Julia's terrific. Besides, she wants to continue living
in Peredelkino, which is fine by me. So we'll have a big
wedding and go on living separately."

"A very good formula," said Malko approvingly, while
thinking that Julia Naryshkin had a real head on her
shoulders.

"What did you want to see me about?" asked Sukhumi.

"Do you know a GRU general named Razgonov?"

Sukhumi put down his Montblanc pen and thought
for a moment.

"Razgonov, eh? Yeah, I think so. . . . Wasn't he in the
Caucasus? I never met him. Why do you ask?"

"Just curious," said Malko. "What about Alexei Somov,
who also used to be with the GRU?"

Sukhumi's face brightened.

"Oh sure, I know Somov. He sold me some weapons
for the Armenians that Russia didn't want to release officially. Somov arranges stuff for buyers who can't procure
them through regular channels. I know he doesn't make

224

a move without a green light from the GRU. But that's business. The generals always need money, and nobody's gonna stick their nose in their affairs."

"Do you know anything more about Somov?"

"He's big guy, nice, speaks a couple of languages. During the Cold War he was stationed in a couple of GRU *rezidenturas*, in Africa, I think. Loves women."

"Do you have his phone number?"

Sukhumi's face darkened.

"Yeah, and I'm not going to give it to you."

The Georgian ostentatiously returned to his paperwork, and Malko understood that he wouldn't get anything more from him.

"Thanks, Gocha."

"Watch your step, Malko. The guys you're asking me about are dangerous. In Chechnya, they used to shoot half a dozen people before breakfast."

Sukhumi paused, and his somber mood passed.

"If you feel like it, come join us at the Turandot this evening. We'll celebrate my engagement—and we won't talk business."

Without waiting to be back at the Kempinski, Malko phoned Julia. It was without much hope, given the way they had parted two days earlier.

She waited until the final ring before picking up.

"Hello, who is it?"

As if she didn't recognize Malko's number.

He forged ahead.

"I owe you an apology," he said.

"Oh, really?" Her tone was icy.

"And I'd like to apologize in person. Can I come see you?"

"No, you can't," she said crisply. "But I'm coming into Moscow for my broadcast, and I can spare a little time before that."

"At the Kempinski?"

"If you like. Four o'clock."

Rem Tolkachev carefully read the report an FSB messenger had brought him.

The FSB had come up with the idea of comparing ballistics data from all the recent murders in the Moscow region. The result was enlightening. The gun found in the burned Lada near the Kursky station had been used to kill both the Igla-S drivers and Anatoly Molov, the KBM inventory manager.

An untraceable Makarov semiautomatic, probably from the Caucasus.

Through the Lada's serial number, the FSB had identified its owner: a Dagestani named Karon Bamatov who had reported the car wrecked in an accident. Finally, the FSB had turned up one intriguing piece of evidence. In the wreckage of the car they'd found fragments of a Diakinov 33 grenade.

Identifying the incinerated body was practically impossible, however.

That was as far as the trail went, but everything pointed to the Caucasus.

Tolkachev turned to the next document, a report from the Moscow FSB. An informer at the Kempinski claimed to have seen a purple Lada pick up one of the hotel guests, a blond foreigner. Shown a photograph, he had recognized Malko Linge, the CIA agent.

Which suggested that an hour before he died, this mysterious Caucasian had picked Linge up at the Kempinski. What had happened then?

Tolkachev had never heard of a CIA agent walking around with a grenade in his pocket. But Linge was the only person who could clear up the mystery of the man in the burned car.

Julia was waiting downstairs in the Kempinski when Malko came back from Sukhumi's. Lacking a magnetic key card for the elevator, she hadn't been able to go up to his suite, and they talked in the lobby.

"I hear you're getting married," Malko began.

She looked at him in surprise.

"Gocha has been talking, I see. Yes, he proposed. I like him, and he respects women. I need a man in my life."

Catching Malko's ironic expression, she immediately added:

"It's for protection, not for sex. It just makes life easier."

She paused.

"I don't have much time. What did you want to tell me?"

"I behaved badly toward you two days ago."

She shrugged.

"Men often behave badly toward women."

She was seated on the edge of her chair, knees together, her coat still buttoned. She was so unapproachable, you could feel it from halfway across the room.

"I was hoping you'd have dinner with me, to give me a chance to explain what happened. Somebody tried to kill me."

"Sorry to hear that," she said. "You live a dangerous life."

Despite her tone, Julia had slightly warmed, and Malko pressed ahead.

"Do you know someone called Anatoly Razgonov?"

"The guy with the GRU?"

"Yes."

"Sure. I used to see him at official dinners in Dagestan with Magomed."

"Is that all?"

"Yeah."

"What about Alexei Somov?"

"Ah, him I know better. He was one of Razgonov's deputies and dealt with the Salafist groups. A force of nature. Over six feet tall, very handsome, loved women. He chased me like crazy. It got so bad that Magomed had a cousin warn him that if he continued, he would kill him."

"Can you threaten a GRU officer that way?"

"Not in Moscow, but in Makhachkala, yes. In the Caucasus a woman's honor is sacred, so Somov behaved himself. Besides, he's not a real Russian. He changed his name. He's actually a Tatar, and he understands Caucasian customs.

"He also managed to keep the Salafist groups in line, even Wahla Arsaiev's people."

"But wasn't he fighting them?"

"Yeah, but he spoke their language. The Federation didn't care what they did so long as they stayed down by the Caspian and didn't make trouble in Moscow. So Somov went to Arsaiev and warned him that if his followers launched a single attack in Moscow, he would kidnap his family, his old father, his son, all of his cousins, and kill them."

"Officially?"

"No, of course not. But he had some Spetsnaz in his group who would've happily cut a *chernozopie* to ribbons for a bottle of vodka and his commander's respect. And Somov was backed by his own superiors. The goal was simple: no problems in Moscow and no independence in Dagestan."

"But there were attacks in Moscow and at Domodedovo Airport," Malko objected. "Suicide bombers from Dagestan."

Julia smiled.

"That's true," she said. "But that wasn't politics, just business. President Astanov was behind them. He was manipulating a little group of fanatical Wahhabists, people Comrade Lenin would've called 'useful idiots.'"

"What for?"

"He wanted a raise in pay. As you know, the Federation sends two billion dollars to Dagestan every year, a country of just two million people. Astanov spreads the money around. Putin doesn't want attacks, and he doesn't want separatism.

"Astanov figured that out. He tolerates the local Salafists so long as they apply sharia law only to Dagestan and don't commit any attacks up north. But from time to time he sends fake terrorists to blow themselves up in the Moscow metro. It's a way of reminding the Kremlin that he needs money to handle his Salafists at home."

Amusing, thought Malko. The Caucasus really wasn't like anyplace else.

"And did Somov know all those people?"

"Of course. He handled them Caucasian style, with targeted killings, kidnappings, and blackmail. Only he was acting on the Kremlin's account, so he was a 'legal criminal,' as we say."

Malko was perplexed. That certainly wasn't the military training taught at West Point. And something told him that the former GRU colonel was involved in the Igla-S affair.

"Do you have Somov's phone number?" he asked.

"I think he once gave it to me. Why?"

"Could you get in touch with him?"

Julia gave him a look both shocked and intrigued.

"Whatever for?"

"I'm investigating a very complicated business," Malko explained, "and he plays some part in it."

"If I call him, he'll have me in bed within two hours," said Julia. "That's how things happen here."

"We aren't quite at that point yet."

Malko hadn't noticed the two men approaching until they were right in front of him. Even a blind man would've spotted them for *siloviki*.

The first one leaned toward Malko and flashed a card with a tricolor stripe.

"I am Lieutenant Pavel Lushkin of the Moscow FSB," he said in English. "We'd like you to come with us, please."

CHAPTER

22

The old Ural truck ate up the miles as Karon and Terek sped along the M6 heading for the Caucasus. The road wasn't bad and they didn't run into too many snags. They were stopped once by a DPS highway patrol, but avoided a search of the truck by handing over a flat-screen TV.

They had elected to take the easternmost route to Makhachkala, through Volgograd. That way, they avoided driving across Chechnya, whose borders were guarded by Ramzan Kadyrov's thugs. The two Dagestanis had no *kricha* there, and you never knew what might happen.

As soon as they crossed into Dagestan they would phone "Pavel" in Moscow to coordinate the exchange of the missiles for the eight million dollars. At that point, their job would be nearly done.

The farther south they got, the warmer the weather. Soon they would be enjoying the balmy breezes off the Caspian Sea.

They were in the Caucasus now, and they began to relax.

The black Audi with the police light on its roof honked briefly, and the gate to 26 Bolshaya Lubyanka silently slid open. The car stopped in the courtyard, and the officer next to Malko got out and politely held the door for him.

"This way, please."

Times had changed since the days of KGB arrests, whose victims stumbled along in the "chicken" position, their arms wrenched up behind their backs.

Flanked by the two FSB officers, Malko was escorted across the lobby, past a guard at rigid attention, and taken up to an anonymous office on the second floor with fluorescent lights.

His escorts waved him to a chair and left. Since picking him up at the Kempinski for what they said was a routine check, the two hadn't spoken to him. Nor had they paid any attention to Julia Naryshkin, acting as if she didn't exist.

Malko hadn't been searched and was wondering whether he should call Tom Polgar. But before he could decide, the door opened on a tall man with cropped blond hair and blue eyes. He was dressed in civilian clothes and was carrying a file.

The man sat down at his desk and asked:

"*Vui gavarite po russky?*"

Malko answered, "*Da.*"

No point in being difficult. The officer doing the questioning knew exactly who Malko was; he was just playing his part.

"I'm Captain Fedrovsky of the Moscow FSB criminal division," he said. "I'm investigating a murder that happened a few days ago. We think you may be able to help us understand what happened. I will witness your testimony, and if you like, you can alert your consulate, Gospodin . . . Linge."

"There's no need for that," said Malko. "But why not just send me a summons?"

"We're in a hurry," said the captain with an apologetic smile.

"What is this about?"

The officer studied his file for a moment, then looked up and said:

"According to witnesses, three days ago you received a telephone call at your suite at the Kempinski from an unidentified man, saying that the car sent by Marina Pirogoska was waiting for you. Is that correct?"

Malko's pulse picked up. He would now have to tread very lightly. The Russians had apparently connected him to the man he'd killed with the grenade.

"That's right."

"Did you know this man?"

"No."

"What happened?"

"The night before, I'd had a drink at Hot Dog's, a bar on the Garden Ring, where I met a woman named

Marina. We chatted for a while, and she told me she hired out gypsy cabs."

That was an open secret, and revealing it wouldn't get anyone in trouble. In Moscow, illegal cabs were practically the only kind to be found.

The officer made a note, and Malko continued.

"She had one of her drivers take me back to my hotel for four hundred rubles, and suggested that I use one of her cars the next day. It would only cost me fifteen hundred rubles for the whole day. So when a driver came to pick me up, I wasn't surprised. From his accent, I guessed he was Caucasian."

"What happened next?"

"We started driving toward the Bolshoy Kamenny Bridge. Traffic was very bad. He wasn't the same man as the night before, so I asked him if he worked for Marina, and he said no. That made me suspicious that I was being set up for something, so I had him let me off in Mokavaya Street. I gave him three hundred rubles and walked to Tverskaya. After spending some time with a friend, I took a different taxi back to the Kempinski."

The policeman was writing furiously. He looked up and said:

"At about that time the *politsiya* at the Kursky station were alerted to a car on fire nearby," he said. "A purple Lada 1500 in a vacant lot. They found a man's body and an automatic pistol with a silencer in it."

"How did he die?" asked Malko, keeping his voice level.

"We aren't sure, but there are signs that a grenade

exploded in the car. He was probably killed by the blast."

"Pretty unusual weapon, isn't it?" asked Malko with a smile.

"Grenades are often used in the Caucasus," said the captain with a touch of contempt.

The way he was talking, he apparently didn't suspect Malko of the murder, which was a relief. Malko decided to go on the offensive.

"I don't know what else I can tell you," he said. "I have no idea what this man did after he dropped me off."

The officer nodded and asked:

"Could you identify him?"

"I thought you said his body was burned."

"That's true, but I'd like to show you some photographs of Caucasian criminals. He might be one of them."

"If you like."

The captain pressed a buzzer and an orderly brought in a big photo album a few moments later. The FSB officer gave Malko his chair so he could sit at the desk to look through the pictures. The album was a gallery of grim-looking men with Caucasian features. Some of the photos were labeled *Dead* or *Apprehended*.

Malko was halfway through the album when he paused at two pictures of a man, front and side views. He was nearly positive it was the killer he'd thrown the grenade at.

"Is that him?" asked the FSB officer, standing right behind him. He had noticed Malko's slight hesitation before going to turn the page.

Malko didn't have much time to think.

"It could be him, but all those Caucasians look alike."

He read the caption under the picture: *Arzo Khadjiev. Born in Makhachkala, Dagestan, on 5 January 1985. Wanted for a variety of illegal activities.*

The captain seemed pleased.

"You've been very helpful, sir," he said. "I'll just ask you to sign a statement. It will be ready in ten minutes."

He left the office with the album under his arm.

It didn't take ten minutes, but an hour, and Malko was starting to feel anxious. When you enter the FSB's offices, you never know when you'll be coming out.

At last, Captain Fedrovsky returned with a stack of papers. Malko initialed each page, after which the FSB officer warmly shook his hand.

"We'll drive you back your hotel," he said.

The same black Audi was waiting in the courtyard. This time Malko was alone in the backseat.

When he got out at the Kempinski, the doorman looked at him with particular respect.

Julia was long gone, of course. Malko was about to call her when he remembered that she would be at the broadcast studio. He decided to accept Gocha Sukhumi's invitation for that evening.

The three black Audis with tinted windows were double-parked in front of 57 Lesnaya Street, a two-story reddish brick building with sash windows and an entry leading to an inner courtyard. The Fishka Bar stood to the left, at number 55. To the right was a dusty-looking wholesale Caucasian fruit store.

The police officers fanned out to check the bar, the stairways leading to the courtyard, and the fruit store, which was closed. According to FSB records, Arzo Khadjiev lived at that address, though the information might be out of date.

The cops gathered in the courtyard afterward. No one in the building seemed to know Khadjiev, but an old babushka coming back from her shopping overheard their questions.

"You often see those dirty *chernozopie* in the fruit store," she said with a scowl of disgust. "Not long ago, they were loading their truck from stuff in the basement, over there."

By then, cops were clattering down the stairs to the store's basement. Its metal door was locked, so an officer took his pistol and shot the lock off. Weapons drawn, they went inside and switched on a bare bulb.

The first man smelled something strange and stopped. Then he looked down.

"*Bozhe moy!*" he exclaimed.

It was a man's body, wrapped in plastic.

Bruce Hathaway practically sprinted for the elevator at FSB headquarters, an escort on his heels. A quarter of an hour earlier, Colonel Tretyakov's secretary had called to ask him to come over to Bolshaya Lubyanka as soon as possible.

It was already 7:15 p.m.

This was surprising, given that FSB agents weren't in the habit of working late. Also, Hathaway hadn't heard from them in days.

The good-looking secretary led him into her boss's office, and Tretyakov appeared a few moments later, carrying a sheaf of photos that he spread on his desk.

"Do you recognize this person, Gospodin Hathaway?"

The FBI Moscow chief could barely hide his surprise. The pictures showed the pale, bloated face of a man with an exit wound above his right eye. His eyes were closed, but Hathaway had no trouble recognizing him.

"I think that's Parviz Amritzar," he said shakily.

"You think, or you're sure?" asked the Russian colonel tartly.

"It's Amritzar, all right. What happened to him?"

"He was shot with a bullet to the neck. His body was found in the basement of a store belonging to Caucasians involved in various criminal activities. Terrorists."

Hathaway turned pale. He had been screwed up and down the line, he realized. Parviz Amritzar, the innocent dupe they had hoped to frame, was actually a terrorist. The FBI had helped him obtain a lethal weapon. And when Amritzar's friends didn't need him anymore, they killed him.

His head in a whirl, Hathaway looked up to find the FSB colonel glaring at him.

"Gospodin Bruce Hathaway, I am arresting you for conspiracy to commit terrorism in relation to an attack in the Russian Federation," snapped Tretyakov. "Without you, those terrorists would never have gotten Igla-S missiles. Those are devastating weapons, as you know."

The FBI chief seemed turned into a pillar of salt. Two stern-looking uniformed officers entered the office and went to stand on either side of him.

"It's too late to begin questioning you," continued the colonel, "so you will be held overnight until tomorrow. Would you like me to notify your consulate?"

Dazed, Hathaway allowed himself to be led to a special elevator and taken down to the second subbasement. A long brick hallway, steel doors with numbers. His guards stopped at number 3, a square cell with a wooden partition, a washbasin, and a chemical toilet.

As the door slammed shut, Hathaway remembered that even when they were caught red-handed, CIA operatives were never treated this way. They had diplomatic immunity. But he was FBI.

Alexei Somov parked the Toyota a dozen yards from the entrance to Marina Pirogoska's building. Night had fallen, and the road was deserted. Somov's wife was away in Sochi and he was driving her car, which was less noticeable than his black Audi.

He walked over and punched the access code into the keypad.

The building had small, ill-lit apartments and no elevator, but it represented a big step up for Marina. In the old days she lived very far away, almost at the MKAD road. Her place was on the first floor.

Somov paused in the hallway and listened carefully. The sound of a newscast came from inside Marina's apartment. The one next to hers was silent.

Normally, her driver would pick her up in an hour to take her to Hot Dog's.

Somov slipped on a pair of fine black gloves and rang the doorbell, producing a shrill rattle. Almost immediately, Marina's voice came through the door:

"*Da?*"

"It's me, Alexei."

The bolts snapped back, and the door opened on a smiling Marina. She was wearing a sexy skirt and blouse with black stockings and high-heeled boots.

"How nice of you to drop by!" she said. "I was about to leave."

"I was in the neighborhood, and I thought I could drive you to the club."

"I'm going to the Bolshoi this evening! I got some tickets that weren't too expensive. But we have time for a drink."

He followed the young woman into the kitchen and when she went to open her freezer, grabbed her neck from behind. His hands were so big, they overlapped as he pressed his thumbs on her carotid arteries, the way he'd learned in Spetsnaz training.

Marina struggled feebly, trying to turn around. Teeth clenched, Somov squeezed with all his might, and felt her body abruptly go slack. He continued squeezing for a moment, then released her. Marina collapsed onto the tiled kitchen floor.

Somov looked around and listened, then left the apartment. In moments he was back at the Toyota.

Access keypads often broke down, so anyone could have entered the building. Because he wore gloves, Somov hadn't left any sign that he had been there.

Feeling reassured, he slipped behind the wheel. Marina had never been anything more than a convenience for him. And he had seen enough horrors in the Caucasus not to be bothered by her death.

In three days he would fly to Dagestan and collect the eight million dollars.

One small concern nagged at him. Before strangling Marina, he should have asked if she'd mentioned his name to the CIA agent.

CHAPTER

23

On seeing Malko come into the Turandot, Sukhumi
leaped from his seat. The restaurant's door was being
held by a bellman dressed as a Louis XV valet, and the
other staffers were in costume as well. Naturally, this
extravagance was reflected in the size of the check.

"They let you go!" Sukhumi shouted.

He rushed toward Malko like a bear after honey, and
his hug was suitably bearlike. Though half-suffocated,
Malko managed to catch Julia Naryshkin's eye. She was
looking very elegant in a low-cut black dress, and seeing
her cheered Malko even more than the Georgian's ursine
embrace.

Sukhumi led him to a deep leather armchair and
shouted to the waiter:

"Black caviar! Lots of it!"

He had already polished off a bottle of vodka, and
now poured Malko a glass and a fresh one for himself.

"*Na zdorovie!*"

That was when Malko noticed the enormous diamond gracing Julia's ring finger. It was about the size of the Koh-i-Noor, only fancier. Sukhumi followed his gaze.

"Meet my future wife!" he declared. "It's a pleasure to have you with us this evening, Malko. Now tell me what happened. Julia said the FSB picked you up, and I was worried. I called my pals, but they didn't know anything."

"It was just for an interview," said Malko. "The Kempinski concierge made a mistake. The FSB people were charming, and I only spent two hours with them."

Sukhumi laughed knowingly.

"Sometimes it winds up being two years!"

The waiter brought the caviar in a crystal bowl and whispered something into Sukhumi's ear.

"He says it's Beluga, from Dagestan," Sukhumi promptly announced. "The real stuff, not that clandestine farmed crap. Actually, it's against the law for them to sell it. But I love it."

The caviar was out of this world, and they dug in.

Every so often Malko caught Julia giving him the eye. If Gocha ever found out they were having sex, there would be blood on the walls.

They continued with blinis, cream, vodka, and more caviar, but began to slow down. You can't eat more than a hundred grams of caviar without choking, and Sukhumi had put away nearly five hundred. Julia was scooping hers up catlike, with a little glass spoon.

By the time they finished the bowl, everyone was full, so Sukhumi canceled the rest of the meal. He got up to go to the bathroom, and Julia immediately leaned close to Malko.

"I was really worried about you," she said.

The look in her eyes said that was true.

"Thanks. I hope I'll be able to see you again."

"I'm a free woman," she said firmly. "Incidentally, I found Alexei Somov's phone number. I hope it's still working."

Just then, Sukhumi's head appeared as he climbed the stairs from the bathroom. Malko just had time to say:

"We'll talk about that tomorrow."

Dinner ended with a creamy Eastern European pastry called a *vatrushka*.

Despite his renewed friendship with Malko, it was soon obvious that Sukhumi wanted to be alone with Julia, and they left the restaurant.

After they parted, Malko's phone beeped with a two word text message from Tom Polgar: *Broken arrow.*

He felt his pulse speed up. The phrase was an old military expression from Vietnam, and little used since. It meant that an American ground unit was in great danger. Coming from the CIA station chief, it had to be serious.

Malko answered: *Tomorrow, office 9 am.*

His night was going to be less pleasant than Gocha's.

Polgar started filling Malko in even before they got to his office.

"The FSB arrested Bruce Hathaway yesterday evening," he said, "and he spent the night in the Lubyanka. The consul went to see him this morning and says he's very depressed. This is the shit storm your friend

Sukhumi warned about. The Russians are out to screw us."

"What are they charging him with?" asked a surprised Malko. "After all, he never got the missile."

"It's worse than that. The FSB found Parviz Amritzar with a bullet in his head in the basement of a store occupied by Caucasian terrorists. And they claim to have identified his killer: a wanted Dagestan activist named Arzo Khadjiev. So they've concluded that the FBI was lying to them, that Amritzar was a real terrorist, and that the whole operation was aimed at Russia."

"What does Washington say about all this?"

"D.C. is still asleep. I warned them last night, and they sent the ambassador to lodge a protest with the Ministry of Foreign Affairs. Which won't accomplish squat, because the Kremlin is running things."

"This is my fault," Malko admitted. "I identified Amritzar's killer. The guy in the taxi who wanted to kill me the other evening. I didn't know that he also shot poor Amritzar."

Malko described being questioned by the FSB, and concluded:

"They must've tracked Khadjiev down by using his mailing address. So what do we do now?"

"I don't know," said the station chief somberly. "But my phone'll start ringing off the hook around four o'clock, and I better have something to tell them. It isn't looking good.

"An Igla-S missile is out there somewhere, and we

don't know where. Maybe more than one. We also don't know what the thieves are planning to do with them. My hunch is that the FSB doesn't know any more than we do, even if they've identified Amritzar's killer."

"Khadjiev was just a flunky," said Malko. "We need to find his boss, the person who put the operation together. And it's all connected to the Caucasus."

"Screw the Caucasus!" growled Polgar. "What I want to know is, can you identify this person?"

"I have my suspicions, but nothing solid. I still think we should give our evidence to the FSB."

Polgar almost choked.

"You must be joking! They'll thank us politely and keep Bruce Hathaway on ice. And that's not counting the threat to Air Force One."

"In that case, I need some time," said Malko.

"Who do you suspect?"

Malko hesitated. The CIA station chief was so worked up, he might go off half cocked.

"I can't tell you yet," he said. "I need a day or two."

"Are you out of your mind?" cried Polgar. "You're working for us, not—"

"That's exactly why I have to be careful," argued Malko. "I'm walking on eggshells. What I'm after is a kind of mirage. I can't risk it vanishing."

Polgar didn't insist. At bottom, he understood Malko's point.

"Okay, I'm going to swallow a bottle of Valium," he said, sighing. "Besides, I have to pay Bruce a visit, and it's best if I don't tell him who's responsible for his being behind bars."

"Don't worry about it too much," said Malko. "The Russians know perfectly well that their trick won't hold up legally. They're blackmailing us. And they'll soon tell us what they want in exchange for Hathaway's release."

Malko sat up when he saw Julia come through the Kempinski's revolving front door. She was wearing exactly the same outfit as the previous evening. When she came closer, he noticed that her makeup was smudged.

"I didn't have time to go home," she said apologetically. "Gocha didn't want to let me go. Can I take a shower in your room?"

"Of course!"

They went up to the suite together and Malko plopped down in an armchair as Julia headed for the bathroom. She emerged a little later, wearing a bathrobe embroidered with the hotel logo. She sat down on Malko's knees and buried her face in his neck. The robe parted, revealing the tip of a breast, which he promptly began to caress.

Julia started, as if she'd gotten an electric shock, and hugged him tighter. Emboldened, he slipped his hand under the bathrobe and continued his exploration.

The young woman untied her belt. Malko saw that her thighs had parted slightly, as if to encourage him. When he put his fingers on her, Julia gave a sigh of delight. She sighed even more when Malko slipped them inside.

Then she eased herself to the floor, shrugged off the robe, and knelt in front of him. As she gently loosened his clothes, Malko closed his eyes. After what had happened three days earlier, he hadn't expected such a welcome, but Julia picked up her blow job where she had left off.

Looking down, he watched the rigid nipples on her breasts brushing against his pants.

When she judged he was hard enough, she leaned back on the sofa and spread her legs.

"Come here," she said. "I want you."

She was telling the truth. This time, it felt like sinking into a pot of honey.

She started moving vigorously under him, meeting his thrusts with her own, raising her hips to take him deeper, groaning open-mouthed until she came with a happy growl.

Which became a cry of pain when they separated.

"Ow! My back hurts."

She stood up and looked in the mirror. She had thrown herself around so energetically, she'd scraped a patch of the skin on her back. Malko felt bad about it.

"I'll have to explain this to Gocha," Julia said, and ran back to the bathroom.

When she came out again, she had dressed and freshened her makeup. She gave Malko a smile both sweet and sarcastic.

"Do you still need me?" she asked.

"Do you really have a phone number for Alexei Somov?"

"Yes. Want me to call him?"

He barely hesitated.

"Yes, I do."

"To tell him what?"

"That you found his number and wanted to get in touch."

"He's going to be all over me, you realize."

"You're big enough not to let him do that."

"You don't know him. In Dagestan a woman once slapped him in public for getting grabby with her. She was never seen again. Word was, he'd kicked her to death."

She paused.

"Okay then, leave me alone now. I'm going to phone him."

A good twenty minutes had passed since Julia had stepped into the sitting room to make the call. To while away the time, Malko watched CNN.

At last the young woman reappeared wearing an odd smile, and came to sit next to him.

"Alexei remembers me very well," she announced. "He also knows what happened to Magomed. He seemed very touched that I should call him and immediately suggested joining him on a trip to Makhachkala in two days."

Then she added:

"If I go with him, I bet he tries to jump me before we even reach Volgograd."

"That's not exactly what I'm after," Malko protested.

"Well, you can tell me what you want me to do, but the guy's a real Cossack, always horny. When he was stationed at the North Caucasus counterterrorism center, all the tribal chiefs used to invite him to their parties, at least the ones who weren't Salafists.

"At those parties they'd have young girls, virgins, dance on the tables. The girls would be given to the honored guests. Alexei wasn't the only man to accept."

Taken aback, Malko said:

"I thought Dagestan was a Muslim country, and very conservative."

"That's right, and the true Muslims were horrified," said Julia. "But it didn't bother some of the tribal chiefs."

The ones who weren't so close to Allah.

"Alexei has guts, too," Julia continued. "I remember I was at Makhachkala when a group of Wahla Arsaiev's followers hijacked a Dagestan Airlines Tu-134 and threatened to kill the passengers. Alexei went aboard the plane alone, to negotiate with their leader."

"Was it Arsaiev?"

"No, one of his lieutenants, a guy whose name I can't remember. It started with 'K.' Anyway, Alexei persuaded the hijackers to release the old people so they could do the *namaz* Friday prayer, then a baby, then the women.

"Finally, he shot the guy in the stomach and retook the plane. President Astanov congratulated him and gave him a medal."

"Was the terrorist killed?"

"I don't know." Julia paused again. "All right, I'm going back to my place to change my clothes. You can tell me what you want me to do about Alexei."

She left without kissing him.

Malko was thoughtful. There was something in Julia's story that intrigued him, but he couldn't put his finger on it.

Tom Polgar looked at Malko in surprise.

"A skyjacking in Dagestan in 2003? Yeah, we must have something on that. I'll call the CIC. They have all the terrorism reports in Russia."

Twenty minutes later, a pimply young man in shirt-sleeves came into the station chief's office with a stack of files.

"Here is what I have for 2003," he said.

He gave Polgar some press clippings and an unclassi-fied report that the FSB had shared with the CIA. It detailed the circumstances and reasons for the Dagestan Airlines hijacking—the plan was to free some Dagestani political prisoners. Colonel Alexei Somov had indeed resolved the problem single-handedly, shooting the ter-rorist.

FSB doctors were able to treat him, and he recovered. Moved by the sincerity of his faith, Somov arranged to have the man join the Yug, a special FSB unit in the Cau-casus. There wasn't much risk in that, because the Dage-stanis hated the Chechens almost as much as the Russians.

Malko noted the terrorist's name at the bottom of the FSB report: it was Arzo Khadjiev.

He closed the file and turned to Polgar.

"We've just taken a giant step," he said. "I think I know who is behind the theft of the missiles."

CHAPTER

24

"**The FSB is pretty sure Khadjiev killed Amritzar,** though they don't know the circumstances," Malko continued. "We know he was also planning to kill me, so he's connected to the Igla-S affair. This is the same Khadjiev who hijacked the Dagestan Airlines plane and negotiated with Somov."

"Who shot him in the stomach," Polgar pointed out.

"People in the Caucasus are forever shooting or blowing each other up, Tom. The survivors work things out afterward. That seems to have been the case here. Somov was used to dealing with terrorists, remember. In the GRU, he was in counterterrorism. We know that the two men got close after the Tupolev hijacking, since Somov arranged to have Khadjiev taken into the Yug group. What happened after that is anyone's guess."

The CIA station chief didn't seem persuaded.

"Somov still has connections in the GRU," he said, "and especially with their number three man, General Razgonov. Those GRU guys are hard-core nationalists, and they're fiercely protective of Russian interests. I can't see an agency like that selling missiles to terrorists."

"That's true," said Malko, "and it makes me think we're missing a piece of the puzzle. But a lot of what we do know points to Somov.

"We know that he knows Khadjiev, who killed Amritzar and tried to kill me. Thanks to Amritzar's cell phone, we also know that Khadjiev was in touch with Somov since early in the Igla-S affair. The stolen missiles were shipped from the storage basement where Amritzar's body was found. And thanks to Julia Naryshkin, we know that Somov is going to Dagestan the day after tomorrow. That's a lot of evidence."

"I'll grant you that," said the station chief, "but the Russians know Somov too. So why haven't they come to the same conclusion?"

"Because they're missing the essential piece of evidence that proves the connection between Somov and Khadjiev: the call from Amritzar's cell phone."

Polgar still seemed dubious.

"I'm going to have a hard time selling this story to Washington," he said wearily. "Meanwhile, Bruce Hathaway is feeling hopeless and the Russians plan to haul him before the attorney general tomorrow. The Ministry of Foreign Affairs showed our ambassador the door, saying this was a serious terrorism matter and they couldn't get involved. They were nice enough to guarantee that Bruce would be treated well, probably put on suicide watch."

"That's understandable," said Malko with a sarcastic

smile. "You look after your hostages. Hathaway is valuable to them."

"What do you mean?"

"You don't imagine the Russians are going to send him to join Mikhail Khodorkovsky in Siberia, do you? They plan to trade him."

"For who?"

"I have no idea, but they'll tell us. You must have a few Russian spies up your sleeve, don't you?"

Polgar was about to answer when his secretary appeared at the office door.

"Sir, you have Colonel Tretyakov on line two," she said. "He says it's very important."

Polgar brightened as he hurried to the phone.

"I bet he's going to say they're releasing Bruce."

But after listening for a moment, his face fell.

"He wants to see me right away. I'm going over there. Will you wait for me? I don't think he'll keep me long."

Malko had time to read a copy of *Newsweek* from cover to cover before Polgar returned, looking grim.

"So, do you have Bruce Hathaway tucked in your briefcase?"

The station chief gave him a sharp look.

"Don't give me a hard time, Malko," he snapped. "We're still in trouble. Here, read this."

He took out a document and handed it over. It was drafted in English on FSB letterhead stationery and signed by FSB chief Alexander Bortnikov. A rectangular stamp declared it *Secret*.

It was a summary of the FSB's investigation of Arzo Khadjiev. It stated that after discovering Khadjiev's Moscow hideout, FSB agents interviewed the neighbors and definitely established that the stolen Igla-S missiles had been stored there before being shipped to the Caucasus. This excluded any possibility of an attack against President Barack Obama's plane.

The FSB director therefore requested that the American government have Air Force One fly to Moscow as originally scheduled. There was no longer any risk of attack, since according to their investigation, the missile was destined for Chechnya for use against Russian aircraft.

Malko put the document down, looking thoughtful.

"So what do you think?" asked the station chief.

"Given what we know, it's plausible," said Malko. "Except for the part about Chechnya. There hasn't been any fighting there since Kadyrov came to power. So there must be another reason for sending the missiles to the Caucasus. Probably business. The Russians have long earned money selling weapons on the black market."

"So the White House is supposed to take the Russians' word for it, without the slightest proof?" Polgar asked sarcastically. "They haven't arrested anybody, and they don't even know where the missiles are. And to top it off, I'm expected to weigh in on this."

"It's tricky, of course," said Malko. "But I think the Russians are right. Caucasian separatists have never attacked American interests. They target Russia and Russians."

"There's always a first time," said Polgar.

"But this isn't it. The guy who wanted to shoot down Air Force One was an American citizen, remember. And we still don't know how he met the terrorists who killed him. If you don't follow up on this note from the FSB, the Russians will conclude that you don't believe them. And that's not going to help matters."

"We're in shit up to our necks," said the station chief. "I'm sending all this to Langley."

"Do that," said Malko. "Meanwhile, I still have a card to play. We'll catch up later."

Driving a Volkswagen with Russian plates—a loaner from the U.S. embassy—Malko went through the entrance to the housing project where Marina Pirogoska lived. He passed an open-air stand displaying cuts of meat on a sawhorse trestle, then a little repair shop. Several other booths stood along the road to the apartment buildings.

He stopped near Marina's building and got out. He realized that he didn't know the access code, but figured he could wait until somebody else went in. He only noticed the uniformed policeman in a *shapka* pacing in front of the building at the last minute.

When Malko approached, the cop turned and asked:

"Who are you going to see, gospodin?"

"Marina Pirogoska."

"You can't go up," said the cop tonelessly. "She was killed last night. Are you one of her friends?"

"Yes."

"In that case, go to 38 Petrovka Street. They'll give you the details."

He turned away and resumed pacing, looking bored.

Sadly, Malko got back in his VW.

His last lead had just evaporated. Who would benefit by killing Marina Pirogoska? Something told him that the murder was connected to the missile business. Marina knew something that she might have told him. But what?

He was sure she hadn't deliberately lured him into a trap. Still, whoever had sent Khadjiev to the Kempinski to take him on a one-way trip knew she was supposed to send him a driver. So Marina must have known that person.

Doors were closing one after another.

Malko had just one last card to play. It was a dangerous, risky one, and it meant shooting the moon. If it failed, he was out of options. And he couldn't play the card on his own.

Julia Naryshkin sounded surprised when he phoned.

"What's happening?" she asked.

"I want to see you. Where are you?"

"I'm at home, but I need some time to get dressed. How about in an hour?"

Just the length of time Malko needed to reach Peredelkino.

Julia was dressed for company: a tight sweater, long flow-ered dress, and high-heeled boots. She sat Malko down at a table set with tea things.

"I'm guessing you're here for some specific reason. Am I right?"

"Yes. I'm going to make you a proposal, but you don't have to accept."

"It must be something dangerous," said Julia, with a gleam of excitement in her eye.

"Not if everything works the way it's supposed to."

"Which it never does."

After a moment's silence, Malko continued.

"Here's my plan," he said. "I'd like you to call Alexei Somov and tell him that you're willing to go to Dagestan with him, but you want to meet him here first."

Julia gave him a hard look.

"So he can ravage me in my own home?"

"No, because I'll be here, too."

This time, her look was one of surprise.

"What do you have in mind?"

"I want to talk to Somov. Offer him a deal."

"Tell me more."

"I suspect he's been involved with terrorists in a really sleazy operation and is responsible for several murders. Also, I think he may have killed Marina Pirogoska."

"Marina's dead?"

"She was killed at her apartment last night."

"Why do you suspect Somov?"

"Because I think Marina could have told me some-thing that would cause him trouble."

Julia lit a cigarette, then crossed her long legs.

"You realize that you're asking me to do something that could put me at risk, don't you? Alexei Somov is a powerful man, and in Russia you don't fool around with the GRU."

"Somov won't be powerful for long, whether he comes to a meeting here or not. I have a piece of evidence against him that will send him to Lefortovo, at the very least. So he won't be able to hurt you."

The young woman took a thoughtful drag on her cigarette.

"I'll have to think about it," she said, though she sounded intrigued by the prospect. "We don't have much time. He's leaving for Dagestan any day now."

"I'll make sure you're in no danger," Malko assured her. "If the meeting doesn't pan out, I'll immediately give the FSB my information, and Somov will be neutralized within the hour."

Malko looked at his watch and got up. He still had to convince Tom Polgar to sign off on his plan, which he'd hatched after learning of Marina's death.

"I'll call you back in a couple of hours," he said. "You can give me your answer then."

Julia stood up in turn, and then did something unexpected. Instead of walking Malko to the door, she came over and wrapped her arms around his neck. Looking straight into his eyes, she said:

"Now that you've got me all excited, I want you to fuck me," she said. Pressed against him, her crotch was doing a silent little dance.

Gocha really doesn't have much luck with women, thought Malko.

Tom Polgar could wait.

The CIA Moscow station chief listened to Malko's proposal without interrupting. Finally he said:

"So what do we have?"

"We have a damning piece of evidence against Alexei Somov," said Malko. "The record of the call made to him by Arzo Khadjiev. The FSB considers Khadjiev a prime suspect in the missile operation, and guilty of several murders. If we tell them about the phone call, they'll immediately arrest Somov. And they have ways of extracting information that we don't."

"That's right, but what does it get us?"

"Nothing," said Malko, "which is why I prefer my approach. Instead of alerting the FSB, I'll tell Somov about our evidence against him."

"So what?"

"He'll realize we have him by the short hairs."

"He'll try to kill you."

"I won't give him the chance," said Malko. "And I'll offer him my proposal in exchange for telling us where the missiles are. That's our main concern, isn't it?"

"That's right."

"Well, Somov's the only person who can help retrieve them. After that, I have a little something in mind."

The station chief listened carefully as Malko explained

the rest of his plan. When he was done, Polgar said admiringly:

"As dirty tricks go, that one's *really* dirty!"

"But if it works, Congress will give you a medal."

"There are a lot of ifs."

"When a general goes into battle, he's very rarely sure of winning."

A long silence followed, which the station chief eventually broke.

"It's eight a.m. in Washington," he said. "I'll send a cable right away, and call you as soon as I get an answer."

"Remember, this is a package deal," said Malko. "It's all or nothing."

Leaving the embassy, Malko practically skipped down the street. Even though facing Alexei Somov alone was going to be like fighting a tiger bare-handed.

Rem Tolkachev reread the text he had written. Addressed to the CIA Moscow station chief, it was what, in diplomatic language, is called a "draft," meaning it didn't officially exist. The offer Tolkachev was making was straightforward, though framed by many considerations, each more dubious than the last.

What it came down to was this: if the Americans didn't want to see Bruce Hathaway tried and convicted of espionage, an exchange "on humanitarian grounds" could be considered—the head of the Moscow FBI office for arms merchant Viktor Bout, who had been extradited from Thailand and was currently in prison in the United States.

The Russian president and prime minister both had approved Tolkachev's text.

Though not a major figure, Bout was a former GRU agent and, more than that, he was Russian. You don't abandon your people.

It was now just a matter of delivering the offer to the American embassy.

Malko took yet another look at his watch. It was 7:30 p.m. The day had passed slowly.

He'd had no news from Polgar, and didn't dare call him. Outside, the Kremlin was ablaze with lights. Nice weather had returned to Moscow.

The station chief called at 8:15.

"Let's have dinner at the GQ Bar in half an hour," he said.

Polgar sounded tense, and Malko figured he was going to be the bearer of bad news.

The usual women were sitting around, their provocative outfits limned by the GQ's soft lighting. Malko was seated in front of a fake fireplace when Polgar arrived. The station chief's features were drawn, and he looked tired.

"Before we start, I need a drink. Meanwhile, read this."

He handed Malko a folded sheet of paper. It was the Russians' proposal of exchanging Bruce Hathaway for Viktor Bout.

By the time Malko gave it back, Polgar had drunk two shots of vodka from a bottle of Tsarskaya in an ice bucket.

"I was expecting this," said Malko. "What does Washington think of it?"

"The president said the idea of exchanging a respected official for an arms dealer was outrageous. Especially in an election year. The Republicans would crucify him."

"So they said no," said Malko.

Polgar gave him an odd look.

"You ought to thank them," he said. "Because of that refusal, they've agreed to your plan. They weren't enthusiastic, but I got the go-ahead directly from the White House. Without that, I don't think it would've worked."

It was now Malko's turn to attack the Tsarskaya.

He was taking on a crushing and dangerous responsibility.

And not just for himself.

It was nearly eleven when he phoned Julia.

"Have you thought it over?" he asked.

"I've decided to do you this favor," she said equably. "I'm coming into town for my broadcast tomorrow. Let's meet at the Café Vesna at three. It's on Novy Arbat, next to Radio Moscow."

So the dice were thrown. Alexei Somov wouldn't pass up a chance to see a pretty woman he was dying to sleep with.

Alexei Somov was in seventh heaven, though physically he was on the fifth floor of the Aquarium, in an office he occasionally used. Good things always come in threes, he reflected. In a few days he would get his commission on the eight million dollars for the Igla-S; killing Marina had bought him peace of mind; and now a woman he'd long lusted after was throwing herself at him.

Somov already sensed that Julia Naryshkin was attracted to him back in Makhachkala, but in those days she was taken.

He looked at his gold Rolex.

Two more hours to go.

He would leave his office at six o'clock in his personal car, without a driver. By flashing his police light, he would be in Peredelkino in forty minutes.

He could already taste it.

Just in case, he took a bottle of Viagra from his desk drawer and swallowed two of the blue pills. He was confident of his sexual prowess, but he wanted to give Julia something she'd never forget.

Their trip to Dagestan together was going to be pure pleasure. It would certainly be the first time he'd fly to the Caucasus with such eagerness.

Malko got to Julia's *izba* at six, driving an agency car with Russian plates. He was carrying a Glock loaded with hollow-point bullets, and wearing a bulletproof vest under his jacket.

He smiled at Julia, who looked very sexy, if a bit pale. She was wearing a fuchsia blouse without a bra, a long, tight black skirt, and high-heeled boots.

They both jumped when the doorbell rang, and Malko felt a rush of adrenaline. Everything hinged on what would happen in the next hour.

Julia stood up but waited for a second ring before going to the door. In walked Somov: six and a half feet tall, shaved head, tailored suit. He gallantly kissed the young woman's hand and gave her a bouquet of red carnations.

"Thank you," she said. "I'll go put them in water."

Julia headed for the kitchen, and Somov stepped into the living room, to find Malko seated on the sofa. He froze, suddenly on the alert.

"What is this bullshit?" he thundered.

"This isn't a trap, Gospodin Somov," said Malko. "I just want to talk to you. I'm a representative of the American government."

"I know perfectly well who you are," he shouted. "You're a goddamned spy! A criminal!"

Just then, Julia came back from the kitchen holding a vase with the flowers. With a backhand slap, Somov sent her and the vase crashing against the wall.

"You double-crossing bitch!"

As Julia struggled to her feet, Somov's hand went to his waistband.

"Don't touch that gun or I'll kill you!" shouted Malko.

Standing just ten feet away, his eyes on the barrel of the Glock Malko was aiming at him, Somov was a fearsome figure, a grizzly about to charge.

If he makes a move, he'll have time to strangle me even if I empty my clip in him, thought Malko.

But Somov didn't want to die. He stood standing, arms akimbo. In a dull, raspy voice he said:

"I'll have you shot!" Turning to Julia, he added, "And as for you, you bitch, I'll kick your fucking ribs in."

A red bruise rising on her ashen face, Julia didn't answer.

With his gun barrel, Malko waved Somov over to a sofa.

"Sit down facing me," he said. "I didn't come here to fight, but to talk. Afterward, you can decide what you want to do."

Somov dropped onto the sofa, his huge hands on his knees and his coal-black eyes fixed on Malko. He looked like a wild animal eager to rip its trainer to shreds. Malko figured it was time to seize the psychological high ground.

"Alexei Ivanovich, I have in my possession a cell phone that Arzo Khadjiev used to call you," he said. "It belonged to Parviz Amritzar, the so-called FBI terrorist.

"The FSB now knows that Khadjiev killed Amritzar, the two men transporting the Igla-S missiles, and the factory manager who released them."

Malko paused.

"However, the FSB doesn't yet know about the call Khadjiev made to you on that cell phone. If they did, you would be immediately arrested, in spite of your position. The phone is in the possession of the Moscow CIA station chief. If anything happens to me, it will be immediately given to Alexander Bortnikov. Are you prepared to listen to what I have to tell you?"

Somov seemed to have shrunk by a good six inches. His eyes were now dark slits in a chalk-white face. If looks could kill, Malko would have been dust.

Silence fell, and it went on and on.

Julia looked as if she were on some other planet. Malko kept his eyes locked on Somov's. The man's hatred was so intense that if he'd had the chance, he would have killed Malko and Julia without a second thought, and without worrying about the consequences.

At long last, Somov spoke.

"So what do you want?" It came out as a cavernous rumble.

Malko tried not to show it, but he relaxed a little. It was like dealing with hostage takers. Once you start talking, the danger eases.

"We want those missiles," said Malko. "The eight Igla-S you arranged to have stolen from the Kolomna factory. They can hit the United States president's plane. Where are they?"

"They're far away," said Somov. "And they won't be hitting anything."

"I can't take your word for that, Alexei Ivanovich. We need to get them back."

"That's impossible."

"Why?"

"It's just impossible, that's all."

Somov had tensed again, radiating hair-trigger hostility.

Malko didn't insist.

"If that's your decision, Gospazha Naryshkin and I will be leaving now. The FSB will get Khadjiev's cell phone this very evening."

He paused.

"Incidentally, I found out how you met him. It was during the Dagestan Airlines hijacking, wasn't it? But I'm sure the FSB knows a lot more about that."

As Somov sat slumped on the sofa, Malko slowly stood up and carefully edged away, keeping the Glock aimed at him. He'd almost reached the door when Somov barked:

"Come back!"

Something other than menace had crept into his voice. Malko turned around and sat down.

"Have you decided to talk?" he asked.

"The missiles are in the Caucasus," he said. "They're going to be delivered to a separatist Wahhabi group in Dagestan. They're never coming back to Moscow."

"That's not good enough," said Malko. "I want to hear the whole story. I need to understand what's happening."

Silence fell again, and Malko went on:

"In any case, the FSB is going to be investigating you soon anyway. Killing Marina Pirogoska was stupid. They'll find out that you knew her."

Malko was bluffing, but from Somov's expression, he saw that he'd scored a point.

"So, are you ready to tell me what I want to know?"

You could have heard a pin drop.

"It was just business," Somov finally said. "When I heard about the FBI plan, I figured I'd use it to get some Igla-S. I knew I could sell them in Dagestan for a lot of money."

"To Wahhabists? You're betraying your country."

"No, I'm not," he snapped, but without explaining.

Sensing that Somov was on the ropes, Malko delivered his final thrust.

"Alexei Ivanovich, I need to know everything *now*," he said, emphasizing every word. "Otherwise there's no deal."

"Oh, fuck it! All right. I sold the missiles for a million dollars apiece. I'm going to Makhachkala tomorrow to get the money."

"What will happen to them?"

"I'm telling you, they won't do anybody any harm. They'll be destroyed. I'm not a traitor."

They had reached an impasse, and Malko figured he wouldn't get anything more.

"Very well," he said. "Here's what I suggest. In a little while, you're going to leave here. We won't say anything to the FSB for now. I'll meet you in Makhachkala, and you'll give me proof that the missiles were destroyed. I realize it would be easy for you to kill me there, but the evidence against you will stay in Moscow."

"How will I find you?" asked Somov.

"I'll phone you. When you give me some solid evidence that the missiles have been destroyed, we'll be square. We won't tell the FSB what we know."

At that, Somov jumped to his feet. For a moment, Malko thought the big man was going to rush him. Instead, he marched out and slammed the door. Moments later Malko heard a car engine roar to life and the squeal of tires as Somov sped away.

Julia came in from the next room. Her swollen cheek made her look like a hamster.

"He's going to kill me, you know," she said calmly.

"No he won't," said Malko. "He won't get the chance."

"I can't stay here," she said. "He'll send people to do the job for him."

"You're leaving with me," said Malko. "I'm taking you to Gocha's place in Moscow."

"What will I tell him?"

"Say you were mugged as you were getting out of your car. That somebody tried to steal your purse."

"He may not believe me."

"I'm sure you'll manage to convince him. Go get ready."

The hardest part still lies ahead, thought Malko. Alexei Somov would do everything he could to escape from the trap. It was lucky Malko held an ultimate weapon over his head.

In his car, Somov pounded the steering wheel, drunk with rage. If Arzo Khadjiev were still alive, he would strangle him with his bare hands. How could Amritzar's cell phone wind up in the Americans' hands?

Suddenly he understood. The CIA agent who was blackmailing him had somehow gotten the phone *after* Khadjiev's death. Which meant he must have killed Khadjiev, though Somov still didn't know how.

His absolute priority was now to get the money for the Igla-S and wrap up the operation. He would then decide what to do. Once the missiles were destroyed, the FSB couldn't accuse him of being a traitor. That was something, at least.

Just then, Somov experienced an odd feeling in his crotch. It took him a moment to realize he was getting an enormous erection.

Then he remembered the Viagra.

By the time he got back to Moscow, his cock was aching. I can't go on like this, he thought. He drove to the Metropol and walked into the bar. There were a lot of people there, including some women alone.

Somov picked out the least ugly one of the lot. A

chubby blonde with too much makeup and a scattered, bovine expression. At any other time, he wouldn't have given her a second look. When he went to stand in front of her table, she gave him a sly look and asked:

"Want to have a drink?"

"No, I want to fuck. Come with me."

"It's three thousand rubles."

"Fine."

Somov yanked the woman upright and propelled her ahead of him toward the elevators.

The moment they were in the room, he shed his jacket, flopped into an armchair, and unzipped his pants. When he pulled out his huge, swollen cock, the woman gaped.

"*Bozhe moy!* You're hung like a bull!"

"You're going to suck me off until I lose my hard-on."

He lay back, eyes closed, wondering how he was going to get out of the jam he was in. He decided he would start with that bitch, Julia Naryshkin.

The blond woman raised her head for a moment, out of breath.

"You're huge!" she gasped.

Somov slapped the top of her head, shoving his cock deep down her throat. She had a tough customer on her hands, she realized.

When Somov was younger, he could have killed a man with a slap like that.

Malko parked and watched as Julia entered the House on the Embankment. She would be safe there.

Then he took off for the embassy, to return the car and bring Polgar up to date. The embassy offices were nearly all closed, but the station chief was waiting for him.

On tenterhooks.

"We're in business!" cried Malko.

But after hearing what happened with Somov, the station chief didn't seem completely reassured.

"He's going to do everything he can to screw you," Polgar warned. "Especially in Makhachkala. People there kill each other at the drop of a hat."

"In that case you still have the nuclear option," said Malko philosophically. "He'll be arrested the moment he gets back to Moscow."

"And you believe that story he told you?"

"Yes, it makes sense. It's the kind of double-dealing that happens all the time in Russia. And Somov did serve in the Caucasus for a long time."

"So how does he plan to neutralize the missiles?"

"Frankly, I have no idea," Malko admitted. "I'll find out when I'm down there."

The station chief went to the bar and poured himself a scotch.

"If we're sure about the missiles, that's all well and good," he said. "But we haven't made any progress on springing Bruce yet."

"Jesus, Tom, you're never satisfied! Anyway, I didn't say this was a sure thing. And now I'm going to bed. This has been exhausting."

"You're sure he won't try to kill you?"

"I'm not sure of anything," said Malko, "but I'm too tired to care."

A lot still remained to be done.

Traveling to Dagestan would be like jumping off a building without a net. In Makhachkala, Somov probably had ten thousand ways to kill him.

A white Jeep SUV with tinted windows was wait-ing on the tarmac next to the small Makhachkala termi-nal. Two athletic-looking men were seated in front. As soon as the Dagestan Airlines Tu-154 rolled to a stop, the car drove over and stopped at the foot of the stairs.

Alexei Somov was the first passenger to emerge. He walked to the SUV and warmly embraced one of the men.

"*Salaam alaikum,*" he said.

"*Alaikum salaam,*" came the answer.

Somov wasn't quite in Russia anymore.

A few minutes later, the car drove out through the air-port fence, respectfully saluted by a guard. Everybody knew that the armored SUV belonged to Rasul Khisri, Makhachkala's new mayor, and nobody would dream of inconveniencing one of his guests.

The SUV drove along the shore of the Caspian Sea and crossed the city to the mayor's waterfront villa. It was a sumptuous residence, midway in style between a Med-iterranean villa and a military blockhouse. A small-wheeled tank guarded the entrance, and walls of sandbags kept potential enemies from assassinating the mayor.

When the car stopped at the front steps, a man entirely dressed in black came out of the villa to meet it. Khisri was almost as tall as Somov, but much more padded. After hugging, the two men went into a living room and sat down at a coffee table.

Khisri opened a bottle of Torkon and filled a couple of glasses. After the brandy was down the hatch, Somov excused himself.

"I have to go take a piss," he said.

The bathroom fittings were solid gold, as were those in the villa's seventeen other bathrooms. The new mayor liked gold almost as much as he liked marble, which covered pretty much everything else.

When Somov returned to the living room, he noticed that his host had set a gold-plated Beretta 92 on the coffee table. Khisri slid the pistol toward him.

"It's for you," he said. "I had three of them made."

Khisri always did have a knack for doing the right thing. He was now observing his guest with small, sharp eyes.

"So, Alexei, is there anything I can do for you?"

"Actually, there is," answered Somov. "Do you still have friends at the army base in Borgo?"

The mayor frowned.

"I do, but the place is watched very carefully."

Somov smiled.

"Rasul, I know you do whatever you like there."

A few years ago, Khisri had set up a clandestine vodka

distillery under some base buildings, with Somov's con-nivance.

"Well, maybe. What do you need?"

As Somov explained the scenario he had in mind, Khisri poured them more brandy.

"That would be very hard to arrange," he said.

"Not for you."

"And it's going to cost a lot of money. At least a mil-lion dollars."

Somov remained unruffled.

"That's way too much," he said. "But just for you, I'll pay five hundred thousand."

"Impossible," said Khisri, shaking his head.

The silence that followed lasted only until Somov leaned across the table and calmly said:

"Rasul, all I have to do is phone the Federation repre-sentative, and your distillery disappears. I wouldn't want to do that to a good friend."

Khisri burst out laughing.

"All right, fine! No need for us to argue. Do you have the money?"

"I'll give it to you afterward. I can't, before."

After a short hesitation, the mayor smiled broadly and said:

"Because we're old friends, that's not a problem. But in that case, you'll be staying here. You'll be in clover."

In other words, Somov would be a hostage. He could leave the luxurious residence only after he'd paid his debt.

This was Dagestan.

"That's fine," said Somov. "Tell me where you're housing me. I want to take a shower."

Before heading to his room, he picked up the gold-plated Beretta, just in case. It was better than nothing.

Lounging in Gocha Sukhumi's Hollywood-size bed, Julia Naryshkin looked at the gray sky over the Kremlin. Her swollen face still felt painful.

Somov must be in Dagestan by now, she thought.

She hadn't heard from Malko since the night before. Gocha seemed to believe her purse-snatching story. Anyway, he was so happy to have Julia at home with him for a couple of days, he would've swallowed anything.

She wondered how all this would end. Not even Gocha could protect her from the hatred of a man like Somov. And if he wasn't stopped, she would have to leave Russia. Sukhumi had some property in Tbilisi, but living in Georgia wasn't the same thing.

Malko had better keep his promise, she thought.

The old three-engine Tu-154 landed a bit short on the sun-swept Makhachkala Airport's single runway. It was one of the last of the Soviet Union's Tupolevs, and the red, blue, and green stripes on its fuselage echoed the republic's flag. Dagestan Airlines was one of the few Russian airlines to still fly Tupolevs, which were starting to fall out of the sky with unnerving regularity.

Alas, every time the Dagestani government budgeted money for new planes, it was embezzled.

Malko joined the deplaning passengers, most of them black-clad women carrying bundles, and a few unshaven, fierce-looking men.

There were no security formalities. Despite appearances, Dagestan was still part of the Russian Federation.

The flat landscape was ringed by mountains in the distance. Malko only had a carry-on bag and was soon out in front of the terminal. He looked around. There were a lot of SUVs, including some armored Mercedes. Otherwise there was little to see besides dust and men in rumpled uniforms. His taxi driver spoke Russian with a guttural accent.

"The Lord Hotel," said Malko. "Prospekt Petra Pervogo Sixteen."

He had made the reservation in Moscow. The hotel was a three-story building with a tile roof, impersonal but clean, a quarter mile from the sea.

The moment he checked in, he left a message for Somov with his room number, 27. Then he settled down to wait. Somov should have reached Makhachkala the day before. He would call Malko as soon as he had proof that the missiles had been destroyed.

Malko was in one of the most dangerous cities in the world, but he was protected. Arzo Khadjiev's cell phone and the record of the call he had made to Somov were safely stored at the American embassy back in Moscow.

Just the same, he had also packed a flexible GK bulletproof vest.

———

The little convoy consisted of two white SUVs crammed with armed men, flanking an old Ural truck. They took the bridge across the deep gorge of the Sulak, a foaming river that flowed into the Caspian fifteen miles downstream.

The vehicles stopped on a kind of esplanade on the far side of the bridge. A short, massive man—five feet eight and 240 pounds—swung down from the Ural. He was wearing a camouflage uniform and carrying an AK-47, a spare magazine, and a couple of grenades. This was Gamzat Azkhanov, Somov's right-hand man. When they were fighting Chechen *boiviki* together, Azkhanov was the one who interrogated their few prisoners. He started by ripping out their fingernails, and later sold their bodies to their families.

Azkhanov now led a small group of soldiers who continued to take orders from the former GRU colonel.

There were very few lawyers in Dagestan. Conflicts were settled with explosives, killings, or kidnappings. The more firepower you had, the more persuasive your argument.

Azkhanov spoke briefly to the men getting out of the SUVs. Three of them carried their sniper rifles up the hillside and took positions in the brush.

He took out his cell phone and dialed a number.

"I'm in position. Do you have the asset?"

Receiving an affirmative answer, he said:

"I'll be waiting."

Two hours later another convoy, this one consisting of three SUVs and a Mercedes sedan, rounded a curve and stopped, facing Azkhanov's vehicles.

For a moment, the only sound was the chirping of birds.

A very tall man with an ascetic face and a long black beard got out of the Mercedes. He was wearing a black shirt and trousers and had a Kalashnikov on his shoulder. It was Karon Abdulahmidov, second in command under Wahla Arsaiev, the man determined to impose sharia law on all of the Caucasus. He was also the man whose death was announced every three months, like clockwork, as a way of earning bonuses for the local FSB office.

While his men took up positions on either side of the canyon, Abdulahmidov walked slowly toward Azkhanov, keeping his empty hands well visible.

The two men met on the deck of the bridge.

"*Salaam alaikum*," said Azkhanov in a pleasant baritone.

"*Alaikum salaam*," said Abdulahmidov.

"The merchandise is in the truck," said Azkhanov.

"The money is in the Mercedes," said his Islamist counterpart.

As one, each headed for the other's vehicle. Two soldiers opened the truck's back doors.

Abdulahmidov had one of the Igla-S cases brought out and opened. He picked up the missile and examined it carefully. It was brand-new, fresh from the factory. He did the same with the seven others, which were then reloaded onto the truck.

For his part, Azkhanov counted the packages of hundred-dollar bills, studying the currency. He also rummaged in the bottom of the bags to make sure some prankster hadn't hidden a grenade under the money.

Their inspections finished, the two men came together again.

"Fine," they said.

Two of Abdulahmidov's men came over, carrying the plastic bags full of currency.

"You can have the truck," said Azkhanov graciously.

While the money was being loaded into one of the white SUVs, an Islamist got behind the wheel of the Ural.

The snipers came down from their hide sites. The exchange hadn't taken more than ten minutes from start to finish.

The Mercedes and the three SUVs turned around to head toward Makhachkala. Wahla Arziev's camp was near Krasnoyarmskoy, north of the city.

Azkhanov and his men turned around as well and headed back to their base.

While still a few miles from the capital, under a clear blue sky and with the wave-tossed Caspian off to the left,

Abdulahmidov's convoy slowed at the level crossing of an abandoned rail line leading to the harbor.

The Mercedes and the first SUV crossed the tracks safely, but when the Ural reached them, a terrific explosion occurred. It came from a 550-pound FAB-250 bomb that had been buried in a tunnel under the berm the night before.

The truck and its cargo were annihilated, and the two SUVs incinerated in a ball of fire. Hurled against a tree by the blast, the Mercedes exploded like a ripe pineapple, strewing its passengers' body parts across the landscape.

A few minutes later, a white Samara appeared on the Makhachkala road and stopped by the railroad tracks. Four men in balaclavas got out and fired Kalashnikovs at anything that was still moving, then climbed back in and drove away.

Malko heard a dull explosion from somewhere north of the city but didn't know what it was. He was starting to get restless when his old Soviet-style room telephone clattered.

The front desk clerk simply said:

"There's someone here to see you."

Two men in a white SUV were waiting for him. He was waved aboard and driven along Prospekt Petra Pervogo to a sumptuous seaside villa with a small tank parked outside, surrounded by sandbags.

The SUV drove into a courtyard and parked amid a number of similar vehicles.

Waiting for him in a marbled living room on the ground floor was a tall, burly man with a shaved head: Alexei Somov.

He led Malko into a little office.

Without bothering to sit down, Somov asked:

"Did you hear the explosion?"

"I think so," said Malko. "What was it?"

"It was what I promised I would do."

Somov explained how the missiles had been destroyed. The way it was done, nobody would be able to identify who placed the bomb.

"Now we're even," said Somov. "I can count on your silence, I assume."

"Absolutely," said Malko. "But I can't make any promises as far as the FSB is concerned. They'll continue their investigation."

"What's that supposed to mean?"

"It means I'm afraid you may be arrested when you go back to Moscow," said Malko smoothly. "After your trip here and the explosion destroying the missiles, they're bound to come to an unfortunate conclusion. And you know what those FSB agents are like. After a few weeks in Lefortovo, you'll be confessing that you smothered your mother."

Somov seemed to have turned into a solid block of hatred. Malko could see his hands clenching, as if to strangle him.

"I'm gonna kill you, you dog," he rumbled.

"That won't help your situation," said Malko. "And it's stupid to wind up in a Lefortovo cell when you've got eight million dollars. I have something better to suggest."

"What's that?"

"Political asylum in the United States. When you get to Moscow, you can seek refuge in the American embassy with your money. You'll be given a passport, and you'll be able to travel wherever you like."

Somov clearly hadn't been expecting anything like that. He swayed on his feet, as if a little dizzy, before speaking.

"Why would the United States do that?"

"I think the CIA would find debriefing you very enlightening. And you'd never have to set foot in Russia again."

Somov took a moment before answering.

"I have to think about it. I'm leaving tomorrow morning. I'll be back in Moscow around ten thirty."

"Think it over," said Malko. "I'll be waiting at the north gate of the embassy at noon."

Without waiting for an answer, Malko left the office and climbed back into the SUV that had brought him to the villa. He had no time to waste. His flight to Moscow was leaving in an hour and a half.

Tom Polgar looked at his watch. To Malko, he said,

"All right, go ahead."

The CIA station chief had met Malko's flight from Dagestan the evening before. From the Makhachkala FSB, Polgar had learned that the Igla-S had been destroyed. That was one problem solved. But Bruce Hathaway was still locked up in the Lubyanka, and the president was threatening not to come to Moscow if he wasn't released. It was the Cold War all over again.

Malko stood up and walked to the north gate's inner courtyard.

The Marine guards had been alerted, so they weren't surprised to see him go out by the pedestrian gate. The street leading to the Garden Ring was deserted. Out on the sidewalk, Malko prepared to wait. Fortunately, the temperature was mild.

His stomach in knots, Malko watched the street corner, trying to figure the odds of Somov taking his advice. He had painted the situation as more dire than it actually was. Somov was an influential figure, and aside from Khadjiev's cell phone, the FSB didn't have any real evidence against him.

Malko was so preoccupied by his anxiety, he didn't notice the time passing.

It was twenty minutes past noon when a black Audi with tinted windows turned the corner, slowed, and stopped next to the fence. The driver's-side window came down, revealing Somov's hard face.

Malko immediately waved to the Marine on guard, who lowered the spiked barrier and opened the gate.

Rem Tolkachev had just received an urgent—and astonishing—message from FSB chief Alexander Bortnikov. Thomas Polgar, the CIA station chief, had given

Bortnikov proof that ex-GRU colonel Alexei Somov was involved in stealing the Igla-S while protected by General Anatoly Razgonov, the number three man at the GRU. In addition to the theft of the missiles, Somov had committed or arranged a number of murders.

All for eight million dollars.

And now Somov had taken refuge at the American embassy under somewhat confusing circumstances.

To resolve this unfortunate affair, the U.S. government was offering a swap: it would give up Alexei Somov in exchange for Bruce Hathaway.

As powerful as he was, Tolkachev couldn't make such a decision on his own.

He promptly called the president's secretary, requesting an urgent meeting. He picked up the Igla file and headed for the second floor, where the president had his office.

"We've obtained a safe conduct for you," Polgar told Somov. "We're leaving for Sheremetyevo in fifteen minutes so you can catch the American Airlines flight for New York."

Somov glowered at him distrustfully.

"How do I know this isn't a trap?"

"You'll be traveling in the ambassador's vehicle, which is covered by diplomatic immunity," said Polgar. "You'll be driven right to the airplane door, and I'll be with you until the very last minute."

Somov gave a grunt of relief.

"Okay, let's go."

A Cadillac displaying the Stars and Stripes on its front left fender was waiting in the courtyard, a driver at the wheel. Somov loaded two big suitcases into the trunk. One of them contained $7.5 million. The mayor of Makhachkala had been paid his cut.

Polgar sat in front with the driver and Malko got in the back next to Somov. The two men ostentatiously ignored each other.

The long car emerged from the embassy and drove onto the Garden Ring. A few minutes later it took Tverskaya Street near Mayakovsky Square, then swung left onto Leningradsky Avenue toward Sheremetyevo Airport.

For about ten minutes, nothing happened. Then, on a long straight section of the highway, a half-dozen black Audis with lights flashing appeared behind the Cadillac and surrounded it, stopping all traffic.

Somov jerked upright in his seat.

"What the fuck?" he yelled.

One of the Audis drew alongside. Through an open window, a man waved the Cadillac over to a gas station on the right. It must have been cleared, because there wasn't a customer in sight.

The moment the Cadillac stopped, a group of grim-faced men approached and yanked the doors open.

One of them flashed an FSB badge—gold letters on a maroon background—and loudly announced:

"Alexei Ivanovich Somov, you're under arrest. Get out!"

He was holding an automatic in his right hand, and looked as if he were itching to fill Somov full of lead.

White as a sheet, Somov turned to Malko.

"You lying son of a bitch!"

It wasn't the most comfortable moment of Malko's life.

"You shouldn't threaten to beat women," he said.

The FSB agents hauled Somov out of the car and dragged him to an Audi. He was bent over, his arms painfully twisted behind his back.

Another FSB agent went to stand next to the Cadillac's trunk.

"The luggage, please," he said evenly.

The two suitcases were moved to an Audi, and the FSB convoy took off, cutting across traffic to the center lane and imperiously sounding their special sirens.

Polgar walked over to Malko.

"Just one word," he said: "Congratulations! I never thought this would work. Let's get back to the embassy. Bruce should be released within the hour."

In the Cadillac, Polgar flashed Malko a wolfish grin.

"Those FBI boys should kiss our asses for the next five generations," he said. "Without us, their boss would have been shipped off to Siberia."

Malko got the feeling that was what gave the station chief the most satisfaction. Personally, he was eager to tell Julia Naryshkin that she was no longer in danger of being kicked to death.

About the Translator

William Rodarmor (1942–) is a French literary translator of some forty books, including five Malko Linge thrillers for Vintage: *The Madmen of Benghazi*, *Chaos in Kabul*, *Revenge of the Kremlin*, *Lord of the Swallows*, and *Surface to Air*. A magazine writer and editor, Rodarmor has won the Lewis Galantière Award from the American Translators Association and been a fellow at the Banff International Literary Translation Centre. For years he worked as a contract interpreter for the U.S. State Department.